Tweaks

The Beginning

By Terry Deighton

This is a work of fiction. Names, characters, organizations, places, events, and incidents are products of the author's imagination.

Visit www.amazon.com/author/terrydeighton
www.tweaksthebeginning.wordpress.com

ISBN-13: 978-1533241429
ISBN-10: 1533241422

Printed in the United States of America

Acknowledgements:

Few books are truly written by one person. I'd like to thank all those who had a hand in tweaking this story. Liz Adair made me think I could write a book. Liz, Ann Acton, Tanya Parker Mills, Bonnie Harris, and Christine Thackeray gave invaluable suggestions. My husband, Al, put up with hours of neglect. Beta readers helped to polish the "final" version, including Dorine White, Miss (Crystal) Deighton and her go time sixth graders, and some who read it so long ago I don't remember who you are, but I took your suggestions seriously. To all of you, thank you.

I owe you.

Chapter 1

Henry Johnson came to a dead stop on the school soccer field. How could Chuck Messer's voice taunt him like that when the bully hadn't opened his mouth? Had Chuckles taken up ventriloquism?

Henry had dribbled the soccer ball across the playfield and sent the ball careening toward the goal, urging it on silently. *Get in there. For once, let me score.*

That's when Chuck had materialized right in front of him and blocked Henry's shot with his thick head. Peering at the school bully, Henry could have sworn he had heard the larger boy's singsong voice.

"Take that."

Squinting, Henry tilted his head. The big jerk's lips still didn't move, but the voice registered in Henry's brain again.

"You little twerp!"

Henry remained frozen in the middle of the field, shaking his head to clear it. His eyes grew wide, and his breath came in shallow pants. How could this be? Peering up into Chuck's face, he searched for some clue as to what was happening to him.

1

Sneering, Chuck cocked his right leg. With perfect follow through, he sent the ball hurtling toward his teammate and fellow terrorist, Bruce "the Bruiser" Crossley. Bruce stopped the ball with his shoulder and moved it downfield, deftly avoiding all of Henry's teammates. At the penalty line, Bruiser paused then drilled the ball toward the goal. Henry held his breath as his best friend, goalie Jim Forbes, dove sideways, reaching for the ball with his gloved hand. At the last second, the ball deflected away from the goal as the shriek of the bell signaled the end of recess.

A groan went up from the soccer players. Jim jogged forward past a bunch of girls, who'd been watching the game. Henry looked closer. Sure enough, one of them was Shandra Powell. She'd seen him standing on the field like a lost kid at the zoo.

"Hey," Jim said, but Henry only kicked at a tuft of grass. Even Jim wouldn't believe what he'd heard—no, what he thought he'd heard. It had to be his imagination. Even so, it had frozen him on the spot, and he'd missed his chance to get the ball back. He swallowed his embarrassment. "Nice save, Jimbo."

"Thanks. I was sure I'd missed it. Then it went zinging off. I guess I didn't feel it through the gloves."

Henry nodded and quickly changed the subject. "How can recess be over already?"

"Beats me." Jim snorted. "But lunch time dragged on forever."

Jim punched Henry in the arm, their buddy code for "race you," and took off running. Henry could never catch his friend, but he sprinted after him out of habit and reached the sixth-grade line a few steps after Jim. He stood there, surrounded by the noise of the gathering crowd, and brooded about his failed goal attempt.

A shove from behind startled him. Chuck's voice, for real this time, exploded in his ear. "Earth to Henry. Move it." Then he added, "Moron."

The others had started walking across the playground. Henry hustled to catch up, stumbling just as they passed by the fifth-graders waiting to go inside. He ducked his head when he noticed Shandra's auburn hair.

Great, she probably saw me almost fall. Stupid Chuck! He always makes me look like an idiot.

The fifth grade line started to move, parallel to the sixth. Henry peeked over his shoulder to see Shandra scowl at the bully. "Knock it off, Chuckles." She wrinkled her nose. "Just because you're the biggest kid in the school doesn't mean you can push people around." She was the only kid at Riverton Elementary who dared call Chuck the name everyone used behind his back.

Chuck shot her a menacing look, but she flipped her hair across her shoulder and ignored him.

As she turned toward Henry, her expression and voice softened. "Nice shot in the soccer game. You almost made it."

3

"Thanks." Henry didn't have time to say anything else with Chuck's hot breath on his neck. He faced forward, blushing, and tried to ignore the volcano erupting in his chest. If he'd known she was watching, he'd never have been able to play.

The sixth grade peeled off and wound around to their side of the portable classroom building and up the ramp. Henry kept his eyes on his feet and concentrated on not tripping. Shandra might be looking as her class came up their ramp on the opposite side of the building. He didn't dare glance over to check.

At the top, Henry looked up into Shandra's beaming face. He flashed a smile in response as they entered the side-by-side doors. Once inside, he hurried to his seat. Shandra had actually smiled at him. The next thought slapped him as hard as if the blow had come from Chuck. She'd probably never smile at him again if she knew he heard voices in his head.

Chapter 2

As the class settled in, Henry hunched over the papers on his desk to hide the goofy grin he couldn't wipe off his face. His mind raced. Shandra would be coming here soon for math group. He wanted to see her, but he couldn't shake the feeling that something had changed inside him—something that made him different—too different.

Chuck's voice broke into Henry's thoughts. "Mr. Goats, what're we going to do now?"

The teacher's steely eyes bore into the class bully. "I've been here a month. I've told you countless times my name is pronounced 'gets.'"

The look of surprise on Chuck's face was obviously phony. "Oh, I *gets* it now. Sorry."

Henry stifled a laugh. Chuck's version of their substitute's name fit Mr. Goetz's long nose and shaggy, caramel-colored hair.

Tapping a ruler against his lectern, Mr. Goetz silenced the giggles. "Let's get started on this week's five paragraph essay. "That's . . ." The teacher paused for Henry and the others to recite with him,

"Introduction with a thesis. Detail. Detail. Detail. Conclusion."

Mr. Goetz adjusted his smiley face tie and shot his best fake grin at them. "I've taught you well." He turned on the document camera. As the words came into focus, Henry muttered them out loud, "What I Have Learned to Do This Year."

Jim whispered his disapproval. "Not again."

Of course, Chuck didn't bother to whisper. "We know what Henry didn't learn to do—play soccer!"

Henry jumped up, but Mr. Goetz got to Chuck first and hauled him out on the porch for yet another talk. Henry dropped into his chair and shrugged at Jim.

Signaling his support, Jim jerked his head upward. Henry nodded back then stared at his desk. If it came to a fight, he wouldn't stand a chance against Chuck's bulk and belligerence.

As their teacher returned, Henry rifled through his writing folder. Before Mrs. Fuller left to have her baby, she used to have them write about their favorite thing to play at recess or why they liked or disliked school lunches. Mr. Goetz's first assignment had been "Why I Am Unique." Every essay since had been a variation on that theme. He seemed to be trying to convince them that they were special. Henry wasn't.

He looked through the folder. Maybe something in it would spark an idea for the new assignment. He came across his "unique" essay. To help those without obvious uniqueness—*like me*, Henry thought—Mr.

Goetz had posted a list of attributes and skills. Henry read through it. Sports. Music. Physical Appearance. Mental Ability. Talents. He'd written the same word next to each—Average.

He had medium brown hair. He stood exactly in the middle when they lined up by height for picture day. His grades were fine but not as good as his mother would like. He could walk without tripping but would never be voted most valuable player on any team. Nothing about him, nothing, was any different from any other small town, sixth-grade boy. That was until half an hour ago when he'd heard Chuck's voice in his head.

He looked over what he'd written about how being so average made him unique. A large red B topped the page with a note from The Goat telling him each person was unique and assuring him he had special talents he hadn't yet discovered.

Now that his gift had appeared, he'd also discovered that special isn't always good. He put the old essay back in his folder. There was no way he was going to write about imagining the meanest kid in the school's voice mocking him.

At least he'd learned a few things this year. He took out a piece of paper and brainstormed a short list, which included the fact that some Native Americans made clothes with detachable sleeves for the summer, the formula for the volume of a rectangular prism, how to do a double scissors fake in soccer, and that Chuck Messer was the biggest jerk ever born. Mr. Goetz would lower his grade for the put down, so he crossed off the last item.

Forty-five minutes later, Henry scribbled out the last sentence of his conclusion.

"Hey," Jim whispered, "wanna come over after school and see my new video game?"

"Can't. Mom wants me to come right home."

Jim grunted. "Tell her you stayed after school for homework club in the library."

Henry glanced at his teacher to make sure he hadn't heard them as he wandered through the room. "She'd know. I swear she can read my mind." The thought struck Henry, and he barely heard Jim's response.

"Yeah, she's got the mom-sixth-sense thing to the max. See you after math."

Mr. Goetz sauntered around a row of desks and faced the class. "Time to clean up. Get ready for math groups."

Half the class got up. Jim and a large group left to go next door to the top math group. Chuck and a few other goof-offs headed to the fourth grade room. Henry and those who stayed with Mr. Goetz dug around in their desks for their math books.

On his way out, Chuck strode around the perimeter of the room, going out of his way to stomp past and "accidently" kick Henry's chair leg.

"Sor-ry!" Chuck apologized in a loud, mocking voice and continued down the aisle.

Henry glared at the bully's back and thought he heard him mumble, "Not."

He swallowed a retort and, instead, busied himself with his math book to avoid staring at the door, watching for Shandra.

"Hi, Henry."

He looked up to see Tina McCray, the sole fourth-grader in his group, sliding into Jim's vacated seat. She wore hand me down jeans a size too big and one of her typical nerdy T-shirts. Today's said, "Q T π."

How could the smallest fourth-grader also be the smartest?

Henry returned her greeting in time to see her wave to someone across the room. "Sit here, Shandra." She motioned to the seat in front of her.

Passing between them, Shandra took the offered seat one row over from and in front of Henry. *Sweet*, he thought, *I can see her, and The Goat will think I'm looking at him.*

Shandra placed her homework on the desk then turned toward Henry. "What's with Jim?"

"Huh?" Henry shrugged. "What do you mean?"

"I passed him on my way here. He was joking around, but when a kid from my class stomped by on his way back from the principal's office, Jim got really serious. From the look on his face, you'd think *he* was the one in trouble."

Henry turned his palms upward and shook his head. He wanted to say something that would steer the conversation away from Jim, but Mr. Goetz's voice interrupted. "Take out yesterday's homework and trade papers."

Henry engineered a three-way swap with Tina and Shandra to ensure he got Shandra's paper.

After the teacher droned out the answers, Shandra turned toward Henry to retrieve her paper, and her hand brushed against his. Goosebumps ran up his arm and got lost in the hair on the back of his neck.

Mr. Goetz drew their attention to the front of the room. "Okay, open your books." He picked up a whiteboard marker and wrote the page number on the board. Henry memorized the shape of Shandra's nose while the teacher chattered on about how to find the volume of a cylinder.

"We start with the area of the base which, for a cylinder, of course, is a . . ."

The class recognized their cue and filled in, "Circle."

"Who remembers the formula for the area of a circle?" Mr. Goetz looked around the room at twenty lowered heads. "Anyone, anyone at all?" Sounding desperate, he fell back on his usual last hope. "Tina?"

Tina slumped in her seat, but she answered, "Pi r squared."

Henry shot her a sympathetic look. Being the smartest kid in the class had its disadvantages.

"Exactly." Mr. Goetz turned to write the formula on the whiteboard. "Where is that pen?" He moved the eraser then fanned through the papers on his lectern, finally finding the errant pen on the floor. After writing the formula in large red letters, he set the pen on the tray. "Okay, following the pattern we've learned for volume, what's next?"

Shandra turned her head and whispered to Tina. "That pen will end up in the trash next."

"Yeah." Tina giggled. "That'd freak him out."

Mr. Goetz pounced like Jim's cat on a twittering bird. "Ah, Shandra, speak up."

She grimaced and then squeaked out, "Multiply the area by the height?"

"Is that a question or a statement, Miss Powell?"

If only Henry could tell her she was right. Shandra took a deep breath and tried again with more confidence. "Multiply the area by the height." Her face colored. She pursed her lips and peered at the whiteboard. Henry clasped his hands together to stop himself from patting her on the back.

Mr. Goetz bobbed his head up and down and reached for the marker. "Now where is it?" He looked in all the usual places. At last, he followed the chalk tray to the end and found the marker in the garbage can stationed below. Retrieving the pen, the teacher muttered, "What in the world?"

The class burst into laughter until their teacher shot them a withering look. Henry flinched under the stare. "He thinks one of us did it."

Tina looked perplexed. "How could we? Nobody left their seat."

Every student but one wore a confused look. Shandra sat perfectly still, staring at the pen in the teacher's hand, wide-eyed and silent.

Chapter 3

Henry dumped his backpack inside the front door after school, breathing in the scent of warm chocolate chip cookies. As always, his mother sat at the snack bar in the kitchen, waiting for him.

"Hey, Buddy, how was school today?" She pushed the plate of cookies toward his customary spot as he slid onto the barstool.

"Same old thing, mostly."

"What does 'mostly' mean?"

"I almost got a goal in soccer during recess, but Chuckles blocked it."

"Henry, don't call him that. I'm sure Charles isn't as bad as you think. I've known his parents since before you boys were born."

"Well, his parents may be all right, but their kid is pure evil."

His mother's brow furrowed. "I hope you're wrong, Henry."

"I can feel him hating me every time he looks at me."

Mrs. Johnson leaned closer to her son. "What do you mean, you 'can feel it?'"

"I don't know. He made an ugly face at me when he blocked my shot." Henry hesitated, not wanting to admit what had happened. Finally, he decided to trust his mother and said, "I could almost hear him thinking, 'Take that, you little twerp.'"

His mother's look made Henry want to take it back. Even his mother thought he was a freak. Finally, she asked, "You heard him?"

"No." Henry cocked his head and wrinkled his forehead. "Couldn't have." He grasped at the chance to sound normal. "Must be I know him well enough to understand the way he thinks."

Mrs. Johnson reached for a small spiral-bound notebook and began writing in it.

Was she taking notes to share with a psychiatrist when she told him her son heard voices in his head? "What are you writing?"

"A grocery list."

He looked closer. His mother used the shorthand she'd learned in college, so he couldn't read it. "More groceries? After all those bags you had me haul in here yesterday?"

"I forgot a few things." She looked at him. "Tell me more about the soccer game."

"Chuck passed the ball to Bruce, who dribbled downfield." Henry smirked. "None of us could catch him. He drilled the ball toward Jim at our goal. Jim dove sideways. He didn't even feel the ball, but it flew off in the other direction." Henry shrugged. "He must have slapped it with the tip of his glove."

"I guess so." Mrs. Johnson sat, tapping her pencil for a moment and then asked, "Was Shandra watching you fellas play soccer?"

"Yeah. Why?" Henry wondered again exactly *who* Shandra had been watching.

"Uh." His mother made a quick note before answering, "It's too bad she saw Jim do well after your blocked shot."

Henry wrinkled his brow and cocked his head. "Ye-ah, that's what I was thinking."

"Hmm." She ran her finger down her list. "I bet Jim felt badly for you, though."

"I guess. Mostly, he was pretty excited about his save." Henry's shoulders dropped. "I don't really want to talk about it."

His mother gazed at him until he started to fidget. Then she gave him a nod and said, "Why don't you get your homework done? Daniel will be home in a while from baseball practice, and your dad should to be on time for dinner tonight."

"Okay." Henry headed back toward the front door to collect his backpack, leaving his mom to work on her list. From what he'd seen, it would feed their family for a month.

The next day at school, it seemed Henry's oh-so-normal life really had taken a turn for the worse. When

Mr. Goetz asked the class to stand and recite the Pledge of Allegiance, Henry jumped the gun and started before the teacher. The class erupted in laughter.

"I could have sworn he said, 'Ready, begin,'" Henry whispered to Jim as they took their seats.

Jim gave his friend a sympathetic look.

A stern glance from their teacher silenced them. "Let's review for your social studies test tomorrow. We'll divide the class in half down this line." He swung his arm between two rows of desks. "When it's your team's turn, yell out the answer." He surveyed each team and then added, "We'll start on this side of the room," pointing toward Henry and Jim's section of the class. Then he retrieved a list of questions from his podium in the front of the room. "Listen carefully."

Mr. Goetz took a breath but stopped as Henry blurted out, "Eastern Woodland tribes."

The laughter during the pledge had embarrassed Henry, but now he wanted to crawl under his desk. The only other person in the room not laughing was the teacher, who stared at Henry with raised eyebrows. Henry braced himself for a scolding. Instead, after several seconds, Mr. Goetz grabbed a clipboard and wrote on the attached paper, muttering something under his breath.

Out loud, he chuckled and said, "That's right, Mr. Johnson. The Eastern Woodland tribes *did* live between the Mississippi River and the Atlantic Ocean. Good guess."

As the morning dragged on, Henry sat in his seat, sulking. When lunchtime finally came, he dragged Jim to a table in the corner. Struggling to keep panic out of his voice, Henry grumbled, "What a morning."

Jim swallowed hard and whispered back, "Tell me about it. I could hardly understand anything The Goat said. I feel so mixed up and . . . and, well, I'm all jumbled up inside, but I don't know why."

"You, too?" Henry put his elbows on the table and cupped his chin in his hands. The thought that he had been trying to suppress all morning couldn't be put down any longer. *That's exactly how I feel, but I know why. I'm going crazy.*

Something rammed into Henry's elbow. He jerked his head up to see Chuckles' leering face. *Losers* resounded in Henry's brain as Chuck turned and stomped toward another table.

Jim spat the words at the bully's back. "The loser here is you, Chuck."

Henry's eyes were wide with surprise and delight. "Did you hear that?"

"Yeah." Jim cocked his head at Henry. "Didn't you?"

"Uh huh, but he didn't open his mouth. I thought I was going crazy 'cause it seemed I could hear people's thoughts. If you heard it too, then . . . hey, did you hear Mr. Goetz ask about the Woodland Indians?"

"No. That surprised me." Jim's brow furrowed. When he continued, it sounded like an apology. "I

17

couldn't figure out how you knew what he was going to ask any more than he could."

"I don't know, Jimbo. The weird thing is, he seemed more interested than surprised."

Chapter 4

Henry's talk with Jim only made him feel worse. It seemed his bad mood was contagious, and Jim had caught it. Now, for the first time in his life, lunch recess seemed too long—much too long.

The sun shone, and laughter filled the air, but a dark and brooding storm raged in Henry's head. He scuffled around the perimeter of the playground with Jim at his side. Henry kept his hands in his pockets and his eyes on the ground except once when he gave his friend a sideways glance. The look on Jim's face depressed him even more. He didn't chance another peek, afraid he might see his best friend cry.

After what seemed like an hour, Henry looked around at the knots of students playing hopscotch, jump rope, basketball, and soccer. Only Shandra stood still, leaning against a wall with arms folded, facing their direction. He turned his back toward her. "Shouldn't the bell have rung by now?"

Jim wiped his shirtsleeve across his face before answering in a husky voice. "It sure seems like it." He glanced at the portable classrooms and then at the playground. "Mr. Goetz just poked his head out the door like he's waiting for us, but no one else seems to have noticed. Even that pokey ol' Oscar kid from fifth grade is playing wall ball. He's usually hanging around waiting for recess to end." Jim pointed toward the main building where several fifth-grade boys were throwing a tennis ball against the wall and chasing after the rebound.

As they watched, Chuck and Bruce ran into view. Bruce grabbed the ball and fled across the playground with it.

Henry shook his head. "There goes Bruiser. He and Chuckles make a good pair. They've each got about half a brain, so together, they can almost think."

Jim grunted his agreement. "Those fifth-graders don't have a chance with those two. Wanna go help 'em?"

The clatter of the end-of-recess bell interrupted. They headed over to line up, cattle-going-to-slaughter-style.

Mr. Goetz stepped out of the portable and waved his arm at his class, beckoning them to come on in. The kid in the front hesitated. Their new teacher had always walked out "with decorum" as an example of the type of dignity he expected from his charges.

Their teacher waved his arm more vigorously. Ashley gave the kid in front of her a shove, and the line started moving. Several of the sixth-graders looked around as if trying to find an escape route. Henry understood how they felt. By sixth-grade, he'd learned

20

that any time a teacher acts strangely, something is going to happen, and, more often than not, it isn't good.

The fidgety teacher seemed to be having trouble containing his excitement, but he only said, "Get out the essays you started yesterday and work on them until math time."

Usually, their teacher corrected papers at his desk while his budding authors scratched away on the week's assignment. Today, however, he paced up and down the aisles peeking at the developing compositions as his students shifted their bodies to block his view. Henry caught snatches of the comments he made as he circulated through the room. "What else? . . . think harder. . . . talents . . . skills . . . special."

At long last, Mr. Goetz looked at the clock with a groan. "Time for math groups. Those who leave the room, line up."

With a collective sigh of relief, they put away their papers. Jim and the others would be able to get away from their teacher. Henry dreaded staying with the antsy man, but the usual tingle raced up his arms. Math groups meant Shandra was coming.

Then a sinking feeling took over in the pit of his stomach, and he studied the stains in the carpet. What if it happened again? He couldn't let her think he was a freak. His only hope was to keep his mouth shut.

When Henry mustered the nerve to look around, he found Tina perched on Jim's chair, swinging her feet. Today's T-shirt announced, "Girls Rule," above a life-sized, twelve inch ruler. She smiled at him and whispered, "It'll be all right."

He mumbled, "Thanks." Did everyone in the school knew about his strange behavior? More importantly, had a certain auburn haired girl with a cute turned-up nose heard about it? His thoughts were interrupted when the girl herself took the seat behind Tina and said, "Hi, Henry."

"Uh, hi, Shandra." Was that all he could think to say to her?

Tina inclined her head slightly towards the teacher. "Why is Mr. Goetz staring at you, Henry?"

As Henry looked in that direction, worry over the teacher's interest entered his heart, and the words, "hydraulic fluid," entered his mind.

Mr. Goetz held up a tennis ball canister, looked around the room and asked, "What kinds of things come in cylinders?"

Someone gave the obvious first suggestion. "Tennis balls."

"Pringles potato chips."

"Canned corn."

"Hydraulic fluid." The words popped out of Henry's mouth before he could stop them. At least no one laughed. Several of the sixth-graders gave him strange looks, and the teacher sported a knowing grin. At least most of the class kept on spouting things that come in cylinders.

The rest of the lesson passed without Henry saying a word. At the end of math, Shandra waited until Tina left and then walked past Henry, leaving a folded paper on his desk. He stared at what had to be a note from the girl who gave him goose bumps. He'd better look before Jim got back. It would be better to be disappointed in private.

"Come to Homework Club right after school in the library today." The hair on his arms prickled as he read. "We've got to talk about what's been going on. Bring Jim." She had signed it simply, "S."

Henry scowled at the paper. He'd finally get to spend time with Shandra, but she wanted Jim there, too.

Chapter 5

After the dismissal bell, Henry and Jim called home on Jim's cell phone to get permission to stay after. They found Shandra pacing outside the library door.

She seemed to have a plan. "Tell Mrs. Melton that you have research to do. We can talk over in the reference corner."

Once settled, Jim didn't waste any time. "What is all this cloak and dagger stuff?"

Shandra didn't seem to mind his abruptness. "Jim, have you noticed anything unusual about yourself the last couple of days?"

"No, not really. I've had a good hair week, but other than that . . ." Jim patted his sandy curls and stuck his nose in the air in a perfect imitation of Ashley from their class.

"I suppose crying at recess is usual for you?" Shandra's tone indicated she didn't intend to prolong things by smoothing over Jim's ego.

"I wasn't crying. The wind blew a—"

Henry interrupted, "Aw, Jim, we were both almost in tears." He turned to Shandra. "That's one strange thing. I . . . I mean, *we* never cry. I've noticed a lot of other weird things happening, too. What's going on, Shandra?" Henry's voice grew louder as the hope for an explanation of his odd behavior rose.

"Shh." Shandra put her finger to her lips. "We don't want to get thrown out of here."

Whispering, Henry tried again. "Well, what do you know?"

"I don't *know* anything, but I am beginning to suspect some of us have . . . have, well, we have some kind of powers." Shandra's face reflected the confusion in Henry's mind.

"So I'm Superman?" Henry couldn't help a touch of sarcasm. More softly, he added, "And you're Wonder Woman."

The sappy tone earned Henry an under-the-table kick in the shins from his buddy. Out loud, Jim asked, "Who does that make me?"

Rubbing his leg, Henry regarded his friend with a critical eye. "Captain America?"

Shandra snorted then leaned closer. "Maybe it's not so much powers as abilities." She looked from one boy to the other. "Henry, tell me if I'm wrong, but you've been getting thoughts from other people, haven't you?"

"Uh." Henry's heart skipped a beat, and a burning sensation crept from his neck toward the top of his head. He took a sudden interest in tracing the fake wood grain of the table, hoping Shandra hadn't seen him blush.

Shandra bent down and peeked at Henry's face and then turned to look at Jim. "Don't be embarrassed, either of you. I don't think you're nuts. I was starting to think *I* was, but now I think it's more that we're developing special abilities." She reached over and tapped Henry's hand. "You *have* heard other people's thoughts, haven't you?"

Still looking at the tabletop, Henry nodded his head.

Jim asked the question for both of them. "What 'ability' do you have, Shandra?"

Her voice betrayed her excitement as she answered him. "You weren't there, but, Henry, do you remember yesterday when Mr. Goetz kept losing his marker during math?"

Henry mustered the nerve to look at her. "Yeah."

"I moved it with my mind!" This time Shandra had to quiet herself.

Henry stared at her with wide eyes. Could this be true? If Shandra could levitate things, maybe he *could* read people's thoughts. Maybe he wasn't losing his mind. Maybe, if his friends had abilities, too, he wasn't a freak.

"Naw." Jim laughed. "Come on, Shandra, what kind of joke is this?" He glanced at Henry and choked back another laugh. "You believe her?"

Shandra didn't wait for Henry to answer. "I can prove it. I've been practicing all afternoon." She drew a dollar from her jeans pocket. "Watch this."

Placing the bill on the table between them, she glared at it with eyes squinted, her mouth pursed. The dollar fluttered as if a breeze had struck it, and then it leaped six inches across the table.

"Whoa!" It was Jim's turn to be hushed by the others. He lowered his voice. "How did you do that?"

"I don't know. I didn't mean to move the marker yesterday, but it seemed funny to me when he misplaced it the first time. Then I started thinking about places it could go." Her shoulders lifted slightly. "As I practiced, I noticed it's easier when I'm emotional."

Henry nodded. "That explains why I don't hear thoughts all the time. It's only happened when I was mad or nervous." Henry took a deep breath then let out a long sigh. The realization he wasn't alone cleared the clouds from his mind. Now he wondered, again, why Shandra had asked for Jim to be there. Henry looked at his friend. "Can you do something, too?"

"I don't think so." Jim shrugged his shoulders then cocked his head.

Shandra peered into Jim's eyes. "I wasn't sure until lunch recess today, but you feel it when other people are upset or scared, don't you?"

Jim sneered. "I don't think feeling bad for my friend rates up there with mind reading and moving things."

27

Leaning toward Jim, Shandra said, "It's called empathy. Imagine being able to tell if the principal is mad at you or only trying to intimidate you into behaving."

"Maybe that could come in handy," Jim admitted.

That explained their lunchtime promenade around the playground. "Now I understand why you were so upset earlier." Henry recognized the range of emotions playing across Jim's face as he worked through denial, acceptance, excitement, delight and then fear and loneliness.

Jim looked back at Henry with gloomy eyes. "Now I understand why we were both so upset." After another moment, Jim gasped. "Ah, gee, that makes me Counselor Troi!"

"Huh?" Shandra scrunched her face at him.

Henry stepped in to explain. "You know, on Star Trek: The Next Generation. She's the empath."

"So . . ." Jim shuddered. "So you get to be Wonder Woman. Henry's Superman, and I get to be a galactic cheerleader."

Shandra shook her head at him. "No, don't you see? You'll be able to tell if someone is lying to you." She winked at him and added, "You'll even know if a girl likes you."

"Yeah." Jim blushed and then smiled and raised his eyebrows at Shandra.

She cocked her head and added, "Or not."

28

Jim shot her a disappointed, puppy dog frown and then laughed. "But it isn't like moving objects with my mind. That would be cool."

Shandra didn't deny she had the more impressive ability. "I'm sure there are lots of things you can do. You'll know when your Mom and Dad are in a good mood. You can get them to let you do stuff."

Seeming to get into the spirit of it, Jim said, "Maybe I can use this in sports. I'll be able to pick out which batter is afraid of the ball, and, Wham! I throw my fast ball right at his ear."

The smile on Jim's face indicated the idea was growing on him. Unfortunately, he hadn't had time to think about the rest of it yet. Henry hated to bring Jim back to earth, but they only had another half hour to work this out. "So we have special abilities, but how did we get them? Who knows about it? What's the catch?"

The daydreams evaporate from Jim's face. "What d'ya mean?"

"There's always a catch." Henry looked at Shandra to see what she thought.

"Well . . ." Shandra pulled her chair closer to the table. "There are a lot of things we don't know. That's why I wanted to talk to you two."

Henry felt something dissolve inside him. Shandra had only wanted to talk to him because she thought he was a freak. She wanted something, but it didn't have anything to do with that strange feeling he had whenever she was in the room. "What do you want from us?"

"I know I can trust both of you, but I think there are more abilities out there." Her face clouded over. "I'm afraid Chuck has one."

"Chuckles?" Henry didn't want to believe it.

"'Losers!'" Jim grunted and then moaned. "Remember, Henry, we both heard it. He can put ideas into people's heads!"

Henry's thoughts swirled. He heard Chuck's voice in his head throwing insults at him like bombs hitting their targets. "Take that. . . . You little twerp! . . . Losers!" It was true. That's why Jim had heard it in the cafeteria. Henry hadn't been reading Chuck's mind that time. Chuck had planted the thought in *their* heads.

Henry turned back to Shandra. "Do you think he knows he can do it?"

"No. He's so used to making people do what he wants it'll take him a while to figure out he has a new weapon."

The vision of Chuck planting wicked thoughts into their unsuspecting friends played out in Henry's mind before Shandra dropped the last depth charge. "There could be others. We have to watch everyone. See who else seems confused or frightened. Who else can manipulate or control something."

Henry shrugged. "Like what?"

"I don't know. Watch everyone, and don't tell *anyone* what we've figured out."

30

Jim groaned. "Do you think Bruce can do something, too? The two of them together, ew, that would be horrible."

"I thought about that, too," Shandra answered. "I don't think so. He's not such a bad guy when he's not with Chuck. He seems to do whatever Chuck puts in his head."

Henry let his mind wander over the events of the past few days. Images came and went, but one kept repeating.

"I don't think Mr.Goetz has an ability, but I'm pretty sure he knows something's going on." Saying it out loud made Henry more sure.

Shandra took out a piece of paper to take notes. "Why do you think that?"

"When you moved the marker, remember how he stared at each one of us? And I'm sure he intentionally concentrated on 'hydraulic fluid' when he asked that question in class. Unless he's like Chuck, he had to suspect I could read his thoughts." Henry turned to Jim. "Did you see the look he gave me when I answered the question before he asked it? Then he wrote something down. Maybe *he's* trying to find out which kids have abilities, too."

Shandra wrote down Henry's evidence. "We'll keep an eye on him and make a list of everyone we suspect and what their ability is. When we know who is involved, maybe we can find out the why and how." She wrote down each of their names and gifts.

Henry raised his eyebrows. Watching Shandra made him remember someone else who always seemed to be writing down what he told her. Of course, she wrote in shorthand and called it a grocery list.

Chapter 6

In his room, with none but his own thoughts, Henry let himself think it through. Coming home late had made it easier to put off his mother's usual interrogation. He had talked on and on about his math homework, and she had finally suggested he go do it.

Now he wondered about his mother. Yesterday wasn't the first time she'd seemed to understand more than she should. He had taken for granted that mothers know what their kids are thinking, but he had to admit his mother possessed that gift in abundance. She bought the exact video game he wanted without him asking. She removed the cartoon character sheets off is bed and replaced them with stripes on the very day he decided he'd outgrown SpongeBob. She always knew which coat he wanted to wear in the morning.

Then he remembered the notepad. He hadn't thought too much about it before, but she always wrote while they talked after school. It had usually been a few words, but yesterday's list had kept on growing as he left the room.

What had they talked about? He'd told her about the soccer game. The note taking started when he told her he could almost hear Chuck. Then she guessed Shandra had been watching without him telling her.

Had she read his mind? Maybe part of the time, but she'd asked about Shandra right after he told her Jim deflected the ball without knowing it. Did his mother know Shandra could move things even before Shandra knew it? How could his mother know about Chuck and Shandra?

"Hey, Hank, dinner's ready," Daniel yelled through the bedroom door.

"Don't call me Hank!" Henry had hated his brother's favorite nickname for him ever since his mother had read *Hank the Cowdog* to him in kindergarten. He knew Daniel used the name to call him a dog without getting in trouble.

As he approached the table, his mother looked up and smiled. "There you are. I was beginning to worry."

"I'm all right. I have a lot of homework tonight." Thinking it best to play it safe, Henry tried not to think about anything but how to find the volume of different three-dimensional shapes as he took his seat.

His father patted him on the back. "That's my boy! Nose to the grindstone."

Henry smiled at him but couldn't help wondering if his father, too, could read his mind. He told himself, *Don't think about it. Think about math.* Better yet, he'd get everyone to think about somebody else.

"Hey, Daniel, how's the high school baseball team looking this year?" That ought to do it.

Daniel took the bait and spent the next ten minutes regaling his family with the facts, figures, and fantasies concerning his sport.

"Jeremy Messer's got a great arm. He's going to take us to state, for sure. Remember how his mom used to blank out to everything around her when he batted in Little League?"

Mrs. Johnson cocked her head. "All the mothers were that way."

"Not like Mrs. Messer. You could hit her with a two by four, and she'd still stare straight at Jeremy with her forehead all wrinkled up." Daniel did a fair imitation of Chuck's mother. "You'd think she was sending him batting advice through the air."

Henry couldn't stop the thoughts. *Maybe Mrs. Messer did send her son messages. If my mom has my ability, then maybe all of our parents do.* He'd have to call the others after dinner.

Realizing Daniel had stopped talking, Henry cleared his mind and concentrated on his dinner. "Great spaghetti, Mom."

Worried she might have picked up on his thoughts, he looked directly at her for the first time that evening. It was time to see if he could read someone's thoughts when he wanted to instead of it happening on its own.

"Thank you." She smiled her appreciation, took a bite of garlic bread, and continued to watch Henry as she chewed.

What are you up to?

Henry almost answered, "Nothing," before he realized she hadn't spoken the words. He'd done it. He'd read her mind on purpose. Had she been reading his? He centered all his worry, all his fear and yelled, if you can yell in your thoughts, *I know, Mom. I know you can hear me.*

His mother sputtered and choked on her bread.

Mr. Johnson turned to his wife. "Are you all right, dear?"

"Yes. A drink will help." Mrs. Johnson took a long drink of water, watching Henry over the top of her glass.

Looking around the table, he realized neither his father nor his brother were aware of anything out of the ordinary. They had already returned to their discussion of batting stats.

Henry excused himself and slipped away from the table. He grabbed the cordless phone and the phone book on his way through the living room. He knew where he'd gotten his ability. Like his brown hair, it had come from his mother.

Alone in his room, he decided to call Shandra first. He had daydreamed about calling her many times, but he'd never suspected it would be to talk about his mother.

Henry's heart beat faster with each ring of the phone. He tried to think what to say if someone else answered. Relief washed over him when he heard Shandra's voice.

He took a deep breath. "Hey, Shandra, It's me, Henry." He lectured himself, *Come on; try not to sound like an idiot.* "I have an idea about how we got these abilities. I tested my theory and proved my mom can read minds, too. And I think Chuck's mom has his ability."

"You're sure?" Shandra's sounded excited. "Then maybe one of my parents has mine."

"Think about it. Have you ever seen either of your parents move something? I mean without touching it."

Shandra laughed. "I think I would have noticed."

She had a point. "But maybe you didn't realize what they were doing. Can one of them stack things up faster than seems possible? Or maybe one of them never bumps into anything. I don't know. Think about it."

Henry paced his room while he gave her time to think. After a few moments, Shandra started in, enthusiasm building in her voice as she talked.

"Now that you put it that way, I've always wondered how my mom can mow the lawn without picking up the sticks and stuff." She paused for a moment then continued. "And she never asks my dad for help to open a jar or get things down from a shelf. I always admired her independence."

Stopping in midstride, his heart racing, Henry lowered his voice. "Keep an eye on her. See if you can catch her moving something without touching it. I'll call Jim and have him watch his parents, too. That probably won't do much good. Being empathetic is kinda part of being a parent. "

"That's true. I think it hurt my parents' feelings more than it did mine when I didn't get a part in the school play."

Henry wondered if he wanted the answer to the next question, but he had to ask. "One last thing. If they do know, why wouldn't they tell us?"

"I don't know. I think we ought to keep it all to ourselves until we figure more of it out."

Henry grunted. "I'm pretty sure my mom's already suspicious."

Shandra didn't answer right away. When she did, her voice carried more than a hint of concern. "We love our families, but I'm not sure we can trust them."

Chapter 7

Chuck Messer awoke the next morning certain of one thing. He was special. He knew it in every fiber of his being. He'd known it for a long time, maybe his whole life. In his earliest memory, he sat on his mother's lap in a big wooden rocking chair, basking in his specialness.

He dressed and went to the dining room confident he would find the exact breakfast he had been thinking of. He didn't usually like oatmeal, but he'd been thinking, as he dressed, how much he wanted it this morning.

"Good morning, Charles." His mother placed a bowl of oatmeal in front of him.

Chuck started to grumble at her for using his full name then thought better of it. Instead, he greeted her the way she had taught him. "Good morning, Mother." He eyed the bowl of pasty cereal. "Oatmeal! How do you always know what I want?"

"I don't. Somehow, you always want what I'm making." His mother ruffled his hair and sat down to her own bowl. "Your father had to go to work early, and Jeremy has a team meeting before school, so it's just the two of us this morning."

Chuck nodded and started eating. The hot cereal didn't taste as good as he had hoped, but it was warm and sweetened, so he ate it.

"I saved the last of the roast beef for your sandwich today. It's your favorite, so I gave your father and Jeremy tuna fish."

He smiled. "Thanks, Mom." It didn't occur to him he had done nothing to warrant the royal treatment his mother had always lavished on him. Even his father seemed to think it right and natural his younger son be given the biggest and best.

Yes, Chuck Messer started the day certain he was one of a kind, and he felt equally certain that would never change.

Chapter 8

Henry got off the bus in front of Riverton Elementary School as he did every morning. He scanned the mingling throng.

Which of his fellow students belonged to the secret club he'd recently discovered? Surveying the crowd, new thoughts came to him. *Maybe some of them have known for years. Maybe everyone has some kind of ability they never talk about.*

Making his way toward the front doors, he spotted Chuck Messer and Bruce Crossley not far ahead. Here was his chance to find out if Chuck had an ability. He'd need emotion and a lot of it.

He crunched his face and remembered Chuck tripping Ashley as she passed his desk. Then there was the shove yesterday. His face flushed, and he clenched his fists. He focused on the bully's thoughts and heard, *Those little kids ought to open the doors for us.*

Henry relaxed and watched. As they reached the double doors, two third-graders each grabbed a door handle and tugged. Standing back and swinging the doors wide open, they held them there until Chuck, Bruce, Henry, and twenty other students were safely inside.

Looking back, Henry saw the two third-graders give each other an astonished look and scoot through the doors, allowing them to bang shut on the next busfull of arriving students.

Henry hurried to the sixth-grade room where Jim was waiting. "Hey, Jimbo." Henry lowered his voice. "I just read Chuck's mind, and I think he made some kids open the doors for him. Shandra may be right."

Before Jim could respond, Chuck and Bruce entered the classroom with a vengeance. Bruce pushed past Milton Freewater. "Get out of my way, you measly maggot." Then he threw himself into his assigned seat.

Chuck growled at no one in particular and shoved the papers off Blake's desk. He watched them float to the floor. "Serves him right for leaving such a mess yesterday."

Henry and Jim busied themselves with the morning geography assignment on their desks and tried to melt into their chairs.

When it seemed safe to be alive in the same room with Chuck, Jim whispered, "I hope you're wrong about Chuckles. He's bad enough now." He looked around the room. "Where's The Goat?" Their teacher always supervised the room before school, and his absence gave the place a vulnerable aura this morning.

Glancing at the door, Henry said, "Beats me. Maybe we have a substitute for the substitute." He didn't dare risk drawing Chuck's attention, so he went back to work. Trying to remember the capital of North

Dakota didn't ease his worry about Chuck having an ability. To make things worse, his heightened emotions allowed his enemy's evil thoughts to bounce around in his head. By the time Henry got to number five on his worksheet, Chuck had taken over half the free world in his fantasies.

Five minutes later, Mr. Goetz rushed into the room with an armful of papers and scrutinized the assembled students. Seemingly reassured nothing untoward had happened in his absence, he strode to his desk and bent over it to deposit his load.

He straightened to his full, considerable height and examined the room again more slowly as he adjusted his daffodil-emblazoned tie. Then he erased yesterday's lessons from the white board, using more vigor than necessary, his shaggy hair bouncing in rhythm to his motion.

More sixth-graders filtered in and began working on the morning assignment with unusual sincerity. Henry stopped writing when he noticed Jim craning his neck to look around the room. He waited until his friend had finished his inspection and then gave him a questioning look.

Jim leaned close and murmured, "They're *all* confused and afraid."

Henry knew exactly how they felt. A strange energy filled the room. Some residual fear exuded from those who had been in the room when Chuck and Bruce burst in, but it was more than that. Kids stole glances at each other with their heads bowed over their work, and their teacher kept wiping the board long after it was clean.

At last, Mr. Goetz broke the spell by turning around and announcing it was time to say the Pledge of Allegiance. An audible sigh escaped from every sixth-grader.

"You'd think we barely avoided the firing squad," Henry whispered to Jim while everyone rose and turned toward the flag.

After the usual morning rituals, Mr. Goetz faced the class. For the third time that morning, his smoky eyes roved from one student to the next, a grim look on his face. When he came to Chuck, his head jerked back, and his eyes opened wide. After a moment, he resumed his survey of the room.

It seemed their teacher was trying to decide which of his students to torture first. Henry strained to catch a clue from his teacher's thoughts, but the charged atmosphere carried bits and pieces of twenty-five different consciousnesses. "Strange . . . in trouble . . . what now? . . . help!"

Finally, Mr. Goetz found his voice. "Today we're going to start a new science unit. We're going to study . . ." He paused, and Henry felt the suspense build before the teacher said, ". . . you!"

The bewilderment of the class showed on the face and in the posture of every student. Henry caught snatches of thought that involved Frankensteinish experiments and horror movies.

Ashley raised her hand and asked the question on everyone's minds. "Is this going to involve bleeding?"

Mr. Goetz laughed. "No, Ashley, no test subjects will be harmed in any way."

Amid giggles and snorts, Jim leaned over and informed Henry that Chuckles was actually disappointed.

Ignoring the class's reaction, Mr. Goetz proceeded. "We are going to study genetics, find out why you are the way you are."

Henry shot Jim a worried look, but the rest of the class seemed to relax in their seats as their teacher continued. "To start with, we need to gather some data. I have a worksheet for each of you to fill out." He projected its image from the document camera. "You'll notice a list of attributes down the left hand side. In the first empty column, you will fill out information on yourself. The middle column is for your mother, and the last column is for your father."

He handed a stack of papers to the person at the head of each row. "Fill out what you can in the next ten minutes and then take it home to finish with your parents' help."

As the papers filtered back, Henry concentrated and picked up his teacher's thought. *This will do it.*

Chapter 9

That afternoon, the three investigators met once again at the round table during Homework Club. Henry had studied the behavior and thoughts of every student he'd come in contact with that day. Some of what he'd learned would make good blackmail leverage, but no one he watched seemed to have an unusual talent.

Shandra got right down to business, pulling a paper from her binder. "Let's compare lists. Did you find others who seemed to show special abilities?"

Henry dug a wadded paper out of his jeans and smoothed it on the table. Jim snatched his from his shirt pocket.

Skimming his short list, Henry wished he had more to contribute. "There's the three of us, of course, and I'm pretty sure Chuck *can* plant thoughts in people's heads. I don't think the kids who opened the front doors for him this morning got the idea on their own."

Jim added, "I watched him and Bruce all day. Bruce does whatever Chuck wants. He doesn't seem to have any ability of his own."

Shandra put a checkmark next to Chuck's name. "I think Tina knows what's going to happen before it does. She ducked just before some kid on the playground threw a ball in her direction at recess."

"Tina?" Jim cocked his head.

Shandra nodded. "She's that fourth-grader in math with Henry and me." She pointed at Henry and then herself. "She's the youngest one I've found. Have you noticed anything about her, Henry?"

Henry shut his eyes to think. He pictured Tina in her typical jeans and brightly colored T-shirt. Today it had said, "Let Polygons be Polygons." Everything about her was short—her body, her hair, her nose. He hadn't thought about her much except to hope she would invite Shandra to sit near him.

What had she said yesterday? After a moment, he opened his eyes. "I guess so. Yesterday when she told me everything would be all right, it seemed like kind of a weird comment. Now that I think about it, she seemed pretty sure of it."

Shandra grinned. "That makes four or five of us. Did either of you notice anything else?"

"No." The boys answered together and then laughed at their synchronization.

Jim crossed something from his list. "I thought maybe Ashley could levitate for awhile, but it turned out she was sitting on a book she'd swiped from Beth as a joke."

"How about you?" Henry turned to Shandra.

"The only other fifth-grader I wonder about is Oscar Newell."

Henry wrinkled his brow. "Pokey ol' Oscar?"

"Yeah," Jim put in, "what do you think he can do?"

Shandra hesitated. "At first, I noticed he never fits in very well. Then I wondered why."

Jim didn't artificially sweeten his assessment. "Obviously, the kid's a freak."

Leaning forward, Shandra asked, "Why do you say that?"

Henry tried to help his friend. "He's so slow. It seems we're always waiting for him to eat lunch. Then recess flies by, and he's at the front of the line waiting to go in."

"No." Shandra grinned. "Lunch is over when it's over. We don't wait for him, but it seems the bell never rings until he's done."

Jim looked at Henry, his faced scrunched. Henry struggled to understand. "I don't get what you mean."

She glared at the two boys as if she thought their brains were clogged. "*We* don't wait for him, but the bell does."

Henry recoiled as if he'd been hit. "He can slow down time!"

Shandra rewarded Henry with a smile. Then she added, "Or speed it up. That's why recess seems so short."

The clouds cleared from Jim's face. "Except yesterday when he was playing wall ball." He looked over at Henry. "That recess seemed to last forever."

Henry nodded his head in agreement. Who would have thought Pokey Ol' Oscar was doing it to them on purpose. Was it on purpose? "Do you think the others know they're doing it?"

"Maybe." Shandra tapped her pencil on the table. "I think Tina has at least some idea, but I'm pretty sure Chuck and Oscar don't."

Jim's eyes narrowed. "If Chuck knew, he'd be causing even more trouble than he is." He curled his lips. "Everyone's afraid of him now. If he makes them think his evil plans are their own ideas, they'll resist even less. Just imagine what he could make everyone do."

Shandra jabbed her pencil at him. "What he will make everyone do, you mean. I think we need to get Tina and Oscar on our side before Chuckles figures out he can have anything he wants."

Walking his fingers across the table, Jim asked, "What are you going to do? Go up to them and say, 'By the way, you have a special ability, and we need you to help us fight the toughest hoodlum in the school?'"

Henry hoped Shandra never looked at him the way she now looked at Jim. Her expression said, "You pathetic child, how do you even manage to get out of bed in the morning?"

Her words were more generous. "I thought we could start talking to them more and hint we saw something special in them. They'll open up once they start to get the idea we're like them, too."

Nodding, Henry took a quick breath. "We've got another problem. I've been trying to figure it out all day. I'm sure Mr. Goetz knows something's up."

Shandra seemed to understand the importance of Henry's theory. "What do you mean? What did he say?"

Jim returned a fair imitation of the look Shandra had given him earlier. "He didn't have to *say* anything. Henry can read his mind, remember?"

Ignoring Jim, Shandra kept her attention on Henry. He shrugged at Jim but couldn't help smiling in Shandra's direction. "He's making a list. So far, I think I'm the only one on it, but he's hoping to find more of us with the science project we started today." Henry realized he sounded surer of himself than he felt. "Anyway, that's what I think."

"What's the science project about?"

The boys took out their worksheets and explained the genetics unit to her.

"That's it!" Shandra ducked her head after her outburst to avoid eye contact with the librarian.

She lowered her voice and went on. "Don't you see? Somehow, Mr. Goetz knows some of us have altered genetics. He doesn't know which of us, so he's using this worksheet to find kids who don't follow normal patterns. We've got to do some research."

They each sat at a computer and spent the rest of Homework Club learning all they could about DNA, chromosomes, and inherited traits. After forty-five minutes of reading Internet articles by geneticists and biology professors, Henry's brain was as muddled as Jim's bedroom. He welcomed the end of Homework Club.

Once they were through the door and in the hall, he pulled his two friends away from the crowd. "Hey, there's still one thing we haven't talked about. If we were genetically tweaked, who did it?"

Chapter 10

That evening, the quarterly meeting of the Riverton
Book Club teemed with tension and anxiety. The club
had been founded fourteen years earlier when twelve
couples met in the Powell home to discuss a scientific
essay written by Trish Johnson, its founding member
and Henry's future mother. She entitled the piece,
"Gain of Function Possibilities in Germ-Line Genetic
Engineering." Six couples had left the club over the
years, but no new members had been admitted. No one
had ever again met the qualifications.

"Something's wrong, Trish." Lydia Powell
glared at the author who had started their group. "I'm
sure Shandra knows something. She looks at me like
she's trying to figure out if she can trust me. My own
daughter!"

Trish Johnson had been steeling herself for
this all week. "Now, remember, we expected this. I told
you that very first night we would have to face our
children someday." Her son had made it clear that
"someday" had come.

Mrs. Messer jumped to her feet. "Of course we
remember, but we were talking about changing the

world and making a real difference then. Now we are talking about our babies."

Oscar Newell's mother regarded the pensive faces of those gathered, once again, in the Powell living room. "Some of these babies are turning twelve years old. They aren't going to be satisfied with simple answers. Oscar hasn't said or done anything yet to make me think he suspects, but he's younger than some of the others, and our ability is less . . . dramatic?"

Mrs. Messer's voice rose an octave as she spoke. "I am *not* going to turn my Charles over to the Institute to be studied like some rat."

Trying to keep her voice calm, Trish said, "We decided that a long time ago." She frowned at Chuck's mother. "you do *not* have to try to put ideas in my head. I can read what's in yours well enough when you're angry."

Trish turned to address the whole group. "I know what I said in the beginning about science being more important than any one person. However, after twelve years of caring for Henry and loving him, I'm no more in favor of continuing this experiment than you are."

"Of course." Henry's father patted his wife's shoulder. "We all know you agree. Everything's been theoretical until now." He faced the group. "We need to discuss this calmly, without accusations or threats."

Tina McCray's mother scooted forward in her seat. "No one is threatening you, Trish. We know you feel the same way we do. I will tell you, though, we'd better have a plan when we leave here." She turned her attention to the others. "I have more than a feeling Trish isn't the only one who is going to deal with this issue. Tina gave me the strangest look when I left this evening."

Jim's father cleared his throat. "Speaking of threats, that new teacher has the sixth-grade class studying genetics. Jim asked me all kinds of questions for a form he had to fill out." His wife reached over and gripped his hand. Her face paled, and she sank deeper into her overstuffed chair as if trying to escape the emotional overload in the room.

Her husband gave her a reassuring look before continuing. "What with the essay topics and his questions at parent/teacher conferences, I think we can *now* be sure Mr. Goetz *does* know something of our situation."

Trish prioritized the issues facing them in her mind before speaking. "I agree the teacher is a concern, but let's deal with the kids, themselves, to start with. Don't tell them who the others are, but if they ask about themselves, don't deny it. We've lied to them enough." Her voice cracked as she thought of her coming conversation with Henry. How was she going to explain all of this to him?

She cleared her throat and went on. "As for Mr. Goetz, I think, for the time being, it would be best not to question the sixth-graders too much about their teacher. We don't want them to give him the idea we suspect him." She paused for a moment and then added, "But keep your eyes and ears open. We don't know which side he's on."

Chapter 11

Henry spent the evening waiting for his parents to come home from their book club and trying to figure out how to ask his mother about their shared ability. His mother strode through the door and planted herself in front of him. He didn't need to read her mind to know she was ready to talk. "All right, Mom, I'm listening."

Raising her chin, she spoke calmly. "I know you have a million questions. I want to answer them all, but I can't open myself to what you're thinking, yet."

Henry unleashed the anger that had built up during the evening. "Do you even care what I think? Did you ever care?"

A sigh escaped his mother's lips, and she sat next to him on the couch. "I'm going to tell you the whole story. Then I hope you'll understand why I can't know your side of it." Henry's father propped himself on the overstuffed arm next to his wife.

Henry looked at his parents and nodded. He didn't understand at all, but he wanted her to go on.

"There's only one thing I want more than to hear your concerns, and that's to keep you safe. I'm afraid I have to distance myself from your feelings to do that.

You'll understand when I'm finished." She took a quick breath. "You know we moved here before you were born when Daniel was in preschool. What you don't know is we moved here on purpose to find a group of people to experiment on."

Henry's father interrupted. "A group of people who wanted to be part of an experiment." He put an arm on her shoulder. "Don't be hard on yourself. We all agreed to it."

Mrs. Johnson gave her husband a tired smile and turned back to her son. "Henry, I'm a world class geneticist. I don't tell you that to brag, but it's important you know I am capable of what I'm going to tell you."

Mr. Johnson moved closer to his wife and put his arm around her. She leaned into him and went on. "I put Daniel in preschool and started studying the other parents. I chose eleven couples who seemed physically and emotionally stable. I approached them one by one and introduced myself." Her eyes seemed to lose their focus. "I explained I could help them give their next child a very special gift."

Henry felt a strange tightening of his chest. This real story of his life, told by the one person whose love should be unquestionable, threatened to shatter everything he thought he knew about himself.

His mother shook her head and continued her story. "In time, they all agreed to meet and discuss my proposal. I wrote it up, so they could read it ahead of time. Then we held the first meeting of the Riverton Book Club. I made it sound so wonderful and progressive. They all agreed to be part of my experiment. It's complicated, and you don't need to understand the science."

Her voice lost all emotion. "I had developed a method that would alter the DNA and enhance a natural talent in each of the mothers. As a single nucleotide polymorphism, the changes should be passed down to our children."

Henry nodded to show he understood well enough, so she would continue.

"I hoped the attributes would be even more evident in the offspring. I required each couple commit to have only one more child in case anything went wrong. Sometimes, a trait kind of piggy backs onto another trait, and . . . and . . ." Her face crumpled in on itself, and she bit her quavering lips.

His mother never lost her composure like this. He watched his father hand her a tissue and give her a hug. Keeping his arm around his wife, he picked up the account. "Three of the children were born with significant defects. They each lived a few hours. Your mother has never forgiven herself. All three of those families moved away, so they wouldn't see the other children grow into their talents."

Drawing a deep breath, his mother continued the story. "Another little girl drowned in a boating accident.

That family moved away right afterwards, too." She gave a slight shrug.

Henry dipped his head to show he understood, and his mother resumed her story. "In order to know if my experiment was working, I engineered an unrelated physical trait that would be passed down with the enhanced ability. Because of that, I know two of the other children did not inherit their mother's gifts. As a matter of fact, those two women are well within the range of normal for their abilities."

She slowed her pace. "The other six of us have developed a skill a little beyond the general populace. You know I can tell what people are thinking, but I can only do it if the person is concentrating on the thought. Also, I have to focus with all my energy. Afterwards, I'm exhausted. I've seen enough to know you surpass me already."

Henry's mother smiled at him, but he could not respond in kind. Even when he saw the disappointment in her eyes, he couldn't bring himself to comfort her. He couldn't keep quiet any longer, either.

"You decided you had the right to mess with our lives just because you could? Is this even legal?" He didn't try to keep the poison out of his voice.

His mother pursed her lips, and her eyes narrowed. When she opened her mouth to respond, nothing came out, and she shut it again. After a moment, she sighed and answered him in a whisper. "It was a grey area." She paused and then went on with increasing volume.

"I thought I knew better than everyone else. I considered myself a trailblazer." She raised her hands and dropped them. "I was a fool."

Henry gazed at her and waited for her to go on.

"You see," she said, sighing again. "The problem is the institute."

"What institute?"

"The Institute for Genetic Improvement funded my experiment. I have sent them reports for the last fourteen years, but I didn't disclose the names of the town or the participants. To the Institute, I am Patricia Lang, my maiden name, so they don't know me as Trish Johnson." She looked to her husband for support.

Henry tilted his head. "Why use two different names?"

"I never told them I used myself as a test subject. All they know is there are six children who might develop amazing capabilities. In my prospectus for the experiment, I theorized the children would become aware of their developing talents during puberty."

Mr. Johnson eyed Henry. "Obviously, it's time for at least the older children to have reached that point."

Henry's mother nodded. "We all knew my test subjects were to deliver their children to the Institute for verification as their gifts emerged. But not long after I signed the contract, I started hearing rumors about the Institute. I began to regret the agreement, so I didn't include any identifying information in my reports."

That explained the notes his mother always took as they talked about his school day and his friends. He felt as if a skyscraper had tumbled down around him, trapping him and weighing down on his shoulders. She didn't care about him; she only cared about her work. He didn't know if his mother read his thoughts or if she was merely continuing the story, but her next comments extinguished his concerns.

"That 'grocery list' I made the other day was the last of my notes. I wrote down the things you told me, so I could go over it again later." She leaned closer to Henry. "I promised the other parents years ago I would never tell the Institute who they are or that the traits had been inherited. I destroyed all of my other records when you were three years old, and I burned my recent notes last night."

The load on Henry's shoulders lightened. His mother no longer intended to use him as a guinea pig. Still, his whole life had been one, big scientific experiment. He covered his face with his hands.

His mother touched his shoulder. "As you grew, I knew I couldn't treat you as a specimen. I love you, Henry." She gently pulled his hands away from his face. "You are my son, and I cannot, I *will* not, let them have you. I am going to the Institute on Friday to announce to them that I believe my experiment has failed. I am manufacturing false data to convince them. That's why I can't talk to you about what you are going through. Do you understand?"

Henry looked up into his mother's face and saw pain in her eyes. "Not really."

"I'm afraid I would speak too much as a mother and not enough as a scientist. They *must* believe I am crushed my work has been wasted. It's the only way to protect you, to protect all the children."

"It's a bit late for that." Henry folded his arms and burrowed deeper into the couch.

His mother brushed the hair off Henry's forehead. "Try to understand. It's breaking my heart, but I have to be able to talk about this scientifically, without emotion, right now. I can't do that as your mother. I want to comfort you and hear all your concerns, but I need you to wait until I come back."

Her husband cleared his throat. "When *we* come back. I know you have to see Dr. Grey alone, but I can't let you make the trip by yourself. I'm sure Daniel can find a friend to stay with, and Jim's folks said Henry could stay with them."

He directed his attention to his son. "You can go home with Jim tomorrow after school. Then we can leave early Friday morning. We'll be back sometime on Saturday. You boys can handle that, can't you?"

Henry didn't know what bothered him more—that his parents were going to leave him when he needed them most or that he had been born as part of his mother's job. He wanted to scream at his father, "What do you care? I'm just an experiment!"

Instead, he mustered a single word. "Sure."

Chapter 12

At school the next morning, Shandra and Jim waited for Henry at the main entrance. Jim looked tired, but Shandra's eyes sparkled even more than usual.

Henry stopped in front of them. "You two must have talked to your parents about 'the *grand* experiment' last night, too."

Shandra nodded. "I don't care what you say, Henry. I think it's cool your mom's a geneticist."

"Maybe." Henry wrinkled his nose. "But will you still say that when we're rounded up and hauled off to some lab to be studied like a bunch of white rats?" He looked at Jim. "What do you think?"

"I think I would do better with unemotional scientists than I did with my mother." Jim's face showed the affects of the sob session he must have shared with his mother late into the night. "She was sad and sorry. I was mad. Then she was mad, and I was sad and sorry. I didn't have anything to be sorry for, but if she felt it, I did, too. I finally went to bed to get away from her."

Shandra looked around at the nearly empty hallway. "The bell's going to ring any minute. Can you meet in Homework Club again?"

"Yeah." Henry snorted. "My parents are going off to fix everything, so I can do what I want." The emptiness of his freedom surprised Henry. He'd always hated having to go right home to report in while all the other kids played at the park or hung out downtown. Now he felt cut loose as if he were adrift on an iceberg in the Bering Sea.

Jim agreed to meet after school, and they headed down the hall toward the back exit. As they reached the playground, Henry remembered something his mother had said.

"There's another trait we all share, a marker that told my mom which of the kids had inherited their mother's abilities. If we can figure out what it is, we can check Tina and Oscar for it before we talk to them."

Shandra's eyebrows knit together. "What could it be?"

"I'm not sure. Something you can inherit from a parent." Henry had been too upset last night to think much about the details.

Jim slugged Henry's arm. "Something like the things on that genetic survey Mr. Goetz gave us."

"Of course!" Henry slugged him back but looked at Shandra. "We'll look it over this morning and tell you what we've figured out at lunch." At least now he

64

had something to say to her that didn't come out all mixed up.

Shandra split off from the boys at the classroom doors, and they entered the portable building as the bell rang.

Mr. Goetz greeted them. "There you two are. I didn't want you to miss our science lesson."

I bet, Henry thought as he took his seat.

After the flag salute, Mr. Goetz jumped right in. "Take out your worksheets. I want you to analyze them with a partner according to the information on the charts I'm passing out." He handed piles of papers to the front person in each row. "Now, first of all, I don't want anyone to panic. Most of these traits come from more than one gene. The 'rules' for eye color are generalizations."

He paused and looked around the room, making sure they were all listening. "If your parents both have brown eyes, it *is* possible for you to have blue eyes. Let's not get any wild stories started about secret adoptions. Now get with a partner and keep the noise level down."

Henry and Jim sped through their work and then went back over the forms together to try to find a trait they had in common with Shandra. Jim had a bent little finger, but Henry's was straight. Shandra's auburn hair contrasted with Jim's fair curls and Henry's dark locks. Jim looked at Henry's eyes.

"I always thought you had brown eyes, but there's a lot of green in them."

Henry nodded. "Eyes with brown and green are called hazel. My mom has them, too." Then he looked into Jim's blue eyes. "Yours have green speckles in them, too."

"Yep." Jim paused. "But both my folks have grey eyes. Do you know what color Shandra's eyes are?"

Henry answered too quickly. "They're deep green."

They'd found it. They all had green in their eyes. Henry tried to remember the color of Chuck's eyes as he pleaded with whatever power in the universe controlled such things. *Please, don't let him have green eyes. We've got to be wrong about him. He can't be one of us.* Henry suddenly needed a name for the group. He couldn't wrap his mind around the scientific gobbledygook his mother had used.

Jim interrupted. "Are you thinking what I'm thinking?"

"How did we describe what happened to our genes?"

"What?"

Henry jiggled his head to clear his thoughts. "In the library yesterday, what was the word we used to describe our genes?"

"We said they were tweaked, but . . ."

"That's it. We're Tweaks." Henry felt better, like his identity had been at least partially restored.

66

"Whatever." Jim looked at him as if he'd lost it for good this time. "The question is, what color are Chuck's eyes?"

Henry tried again to envision Chuck's face. "I can't remember. Go look." Henry felt as if he were sacrificing his friend to an ancient idol.

"Right. Why don't I ask him to loan me five bucks while I'm at it?" Jim backhanded Henry's arm to underscore his point. "Why don't you go look?"

Mr. Goetz saved Henry from answering. "All right, class, return to your own seats, and let's see what we've found out."

Henry breathed a sigh of relief. "I guess Chuck's eyes will have to wait."

Luckily, Mr. Goetz provided the answer for them. "We're going to divide the class by different traits. Everyone with blue eyes congregate on the west side of the room over by the pencil sharpener." He directed them with his arm like a symphony conductor. "Brown eyes are in the middle." Green and grey eyed folks mosey over to the east side by the bulletin board."

Henry and Jim blurted at the same time, "What about green speckles?"

Mr. Goetz peered at them with squinted eyes. "Go with the green." Explaining to the rest of the class, he said, "Some eyes have combinations of colors."

Chaos reigned while everyone moved into their indicated groups. Henry watched Chuck with a sideways glance. Jim planted his back toward Chuck, and Henry assumed he silently chanted the same mantra. *Go the other way. Go the other way.*

Miraculously, Chuck stood and headed toward the west. Could it be? Did Chuck have blue eyes? Forgetting his covert intentions, Henry stared at Chuck's back as the bully sharpened his pencil and turned around. Chuck picked his way around the desks and headed toward the middle of the room.

Jim turned at an angle and watched with Henry. Knowing it would do no good, Henry chanted in his mind. *Stop in the middle. Stop in the middle.*

Chuck kept coming like a steamroller with a mission. He walked past Jim and planted himself against the bulletin board. Henry's stomach cramped. Chuck *was* a Tweak.

Chapter 13

"I *told* you Chuck was one of us." Shandra exited the lunch room, tossing her empty sack in the trash, and took a few steps toward the playground. When she turned back to the two boys, Henry tried not to show the hurt he felt at her words. He must not have been successful because she softened her tone. "I don't blame you for hoping, but we have to face the fact."

Henry and Jim followed her onto the playground before she spoke again. "Now we need to find out if Oscar and Tina are the other two." She turned to Henry. "We can check Tina's eyes during math, but I don't sit anywhere near Oscar in class."

"Wellll." Jim did an imitation of Eeyore's slow drawl. "We'd better check out Pokey Ol' Oscar now."

Shandra threw her hands in the air. "But what are we going to say to him and Tina?"

Jim buried his face in his hands and shook it in Shandra's direction. "I don't know how you girls stand all this emotion." He dropped his hands. "Stop worrying. *I* can't think when *you're* all stirred up."

"Sorry. I'll try." Shandra put a smile on her face, but Henry could see the concern in her eyes. He knew how she felt. Nobody wants to go around telling people, "I'm a freak, and, by the way, you are, too."

Jim must have managed a thought somehow because he came up with a plan. "We could tell them we need some help with a special project for science. We can invite them to come to Homework Club after school today."

Henry gave him a friendly shove. "And you said you couldn't think."

They found Oscar playing wall ball with a group of boys. Shandra pushed Henry toward him, and Henry had no choice but to speak for the group. "Hey, Oscar, can I talk to you?"

Oscar looked over at Henry as the ball struck the back of the school. "What for? I'm in the game." His voice resonated with pride. Henry couldn't help but wonder how Oscar would react to belonging to this new group.

"It'll only take a second." Henry couldn't see Oscar's eyes because he kept them on the bouncing ball. As another boy caught the ball and prepared to throw it, Oscar turned. His light green eyes peered at Henry through his glasses.

Henry talked fast to hold his attention. "Jim and I are working on a science project. We need people with green in their eyes to help us out. Can you come to Homework Club this afternoon for a few minutes?"

"I guess." Oscar dove for the ball but missed and connected with the pavement. The bell rang as Henry helped him up. Oscar brushed off his pants, and Henry shot Jim and Shandra two thumbs up. Oscar ignored them and staggered away, looking slightly dazed.

Jim shook his head. "Oscar must be tired of recess."

"Yeah." Henry followed Jim to their line but looked back at Oscar. He still plodded toward the fifth-grade line, digging gravel out of his skinned elbow. Suddenly, he hit the pavement again as Chuck appeared from behind him.

Chuck bellowed as if he were the injured party. "Watch where you're going. You could have tripped me."

Oscar looked up with green fire in his eyes but said nothing.

Every muscle in Henry's body tightened. Chuck had to be stopped. He took a deep breath to relax. At least Chuck's terrorism would help with the recruitment. Oscar would want to get back at him for that shove.

Chapter 14

Tina's hazel eyes burned with curiosity. "What's this about, anyway?"

Shandra sat next to Jim across a round library table from the two new recruits. "Henry's printing some information we want to show you as we explain. Don't worry. We're not going to hurt you."

"I know." Tina paused for a moment and then said, "It's not you three I'm worried about."

It would be best not to get ahead of the plan by asking Tina what she meant. Instead, Shandra said, "Henry had to prove to the librarian that his class is studying genetics before she'd let him print the information." She whispered to Jim, "Whatever else he's up to, Mr. Goetz helped us out with that."

Tina looked at her without comment or expression, but even without Jim's ability, Shandra could tell what Oscar was feeling. Confusion had taken over every inch of his face. She smiled her reassurance to him, knowing the coming discussion would confuse him even more.

Glancing back over toward the printer, she noticed Henry coming their way. "Here he is now." Shandra tried to sound matter of fact, but she didn't know how to begin. She looked to Jim and Henry. They looked at her as if perfectly happy to let her brave the unknown alone.

She took a deep breath. "Well, we have to admit we aren't really working on a science project." As irritation showed on their faces, she quickly added, "It does have to do with the sixth-grade science unit." She fumbled for a way to explain. "But what we want to talk to you about isn't for a grade." She looked at Henry and begged for help with her eyes.

He took a deep breath. "We've noticed something that makes you two kind of special."

Oscar scowled. "Special how?"

"Have you ever noticed how, sometimes, time seems to go really fast? Then, other times, it seems to go really slow, like when you can't wait for something to be over?" Henry waited for Oscar to think about that.

"No. Time always seems to pass the same. I always have the right amount of time to do what I want." Oscar looked at Tina.

"*I* know what you mean." Tina nodded. "Recess is never long enough, but lunch takes forever."

Oscar's tone indicated a slight grasp on the concept. "Not for me."

Henry took advantage of the moment. "And, Tina, what makes you so good at math?"

Tina didn't need to think about it. "I have a good memory, and I have a sense of what comes next. I get that from my mother."

"Yeah, you do," Henry agreed.

Jim turned it back to Oscar. "I bet *your* mother never rushes like other moms, right?"

The younger boy grinned. "How did you know? She always has everything done right on time."

Henry sprang the trap. "We've noticed some unusual things about ourselves, too. We've done some research and gotten proof from our parents."

In a conspiratorial tone, Jim whispered, "We'll tell you all about it, but you have to promise to stay put and hear us out to the end. Shandra has something pretty cool to show you when we're done."

Shandra took her cue and told the story, starting with the disappearing marker and ending with Tina's green eyes. She used Henry's internet printouts as visual aids.

"Then," Henry said, tapping the table lightly, "we were sure you two were like us."

Tina appeared to be taking the whole thing calmly. "I wondered why you two kept staring at me in math."

However, Oscar shrank away from them, looking around as if about to break and run for cover. Shandra decided the superhero approach wouldn't work. This was a job for Counselor Troi. She nudged Jim.

He seemed to understand her meaning and concentrated his gaze on Oscar. After a moment, Jim smiled. "We know you're worried about being different. We were, too, until we realized we're in this together." Jim titled his head toward Oscar. "There're

74

only six of us in the world, and five of us are at this table."

Oscar looked around at the other four faces. "I don't know. You all seem convinced, but this ability you say I have isn't something I can test. How do I know you're telling the truth?"

Shandra put a pen in the middle of the table. "That's my job." She stared at the pen. It rolled slightly, and then it rose into the air and, pointing at Oscar, moved forward.

"Whoa." Oscar grabbed the pen and shook it. The others laughed and then ducked their heads to avoid the librarian's steady gaze.

Jim stifled one last laugh. "What do you say now?"

"Okay." Oscar put the pen down as if it were radioactive. "Okay, I believe you. Now, what do you want from me?"

Tina stared at him. "Why do you think the sixth kid isn't here?" She didn't wait for an answer. "It's Chuck Messer! They want us to help them fight him. I knew this had something to do with that creep."

Henry looked at Shandra with wide eyes. Shandra nodded in triumph. She'd been right. Tina could sense the future.

"Oh, no." Oscar sounded panicked. " He'll kill me!"

Henry seemed to put all the anger he felt toward Chuck into his voice. "I saw what he did to you today. We've got to stop him from picking on everyone."

Oscar's voice trembled. "How do you think we can do that?"

His fear pricked at Shandra's confidence. They would need all of their abilities to triumph over Chuck. She took a deep breath and explained their thinking. "If he knows we have abilities, too, and we won't let him get away with being a bully, he'll have to stop harassing everyone.

Jim grinned at Oscar. "We'll all be together. We won't let anything happen to you. Right, guys?"

Shandra and Henry bobbed their heads. Then Shandra shifted her attention to the right. "What do you think, Tina?" Shandra nodded slightly to encourage the younger girl.

Tina wrinkled her brow. "I've always had a sixth sense about the future, but recently, it's, I don't know, stronger. Then, the day before yesterday, I saw Henry in my mind as he figured out he wasn't crazy. I didn't understand what I saw happening, but I knew Henry did and that it would be all right."

Her face broke out in a huge grin, and she turned toward Oscar. "If we all practice our abilities, how could Chuckles dare go against us?" Tina had made her choice.

Oscar studied each of their faces in turn. Shandra knew he had never had many friends. She hoped he would be able to trust them. She held her breath as he gave his answer.

"I'll try."

Tina smiled at him. "You'll do more than try, Oscar. You're going to be amazing!"

Chapter 15

Mark Goetz sat at his desk, reflecting in the after-school quiet of his empty classroom. He looked at the clipboard in front of him, mumbling to himself. "That's four. There should be two more. Maybe they're at the middle school." He wrinkled his brow and then thought, *No, it's more likely they're younger. I need to get to know more of the fourth and fifth graders. The ones with green eyes, anyway.*

He opened his email and sent a message to the fifth-grade teacher asking her to let him take her recess duty the next day. He knew she wouldn't need persuading. No teacher this side of crazy would pass up getting out of recess duty on Friday afternoon.

Turning his attention back to the clipboard, he made notations beside each name on the list.

Henry Johnson– telepathy – reads thoughts

Chuck Messer–psychic transfer– plants thoughts

Jim Forbes– empathic mimicry—feels others' emotions

Shandra Powell– telekinesis—moves things with mind

"Thought, emotion, space – what's missing?"

He pondered for a moment and then added Tina's name under the others. Accepted but not really part of the group, the fourth grader had been treated as the math class mascot until the last couple of days. Now she had become chummy with Shandra and Henry who were both on his list. Tina was precocious, and she had green in her eyes. He didn't know what she could do, but he'd bet a year's salary she was one of them.

"Thought, emotion, space." He repeated the words as he looked around the room, searching for the answer, until his eyes landed on the clock. "Time. That's what's missing. Can one or both of them manipulate time?" An inch below Tina's name, he drew a line.

When he figured out whose name belonged on that line and what he or she could do, he'd be ready.

Chapter 16

Comparing the Forbes's house to the Johnson's would be like comparing a rap song to classical music. Henry had not known his mother was a scientist, but now that he did, it made perfect sense. Their clean, almost sterile home reflected exactness and precision. Everything happened according to a schedule. They discussed plans ahead of time and evaluated each detail afterwards.

That day after school at the Forbes's, Jim's mother flitted from project to project and rarely finished anything. The house was clean enough, but it was definitely lived in. Henry didn't feel quite comfortable in the chaos. *I guess it depends on what you're used to,* he thought as he settled into the couch to wait for Jim to do his afterschool chores.

Mrs. Forbes stopped vacuuming to tend to one of the children's needs. Henry wondered if she'd manage to get back to it. A few minutes later, in her foray through the house in search of whatever she had been doing, she stumbled across Henry alone in the living room.

She propped herself against the arm of an overstuffed chair just inside the room. "What'd you do with Jim?"

"He's taking out the garbage." Henry had offered to help, but Jim said he wanted a few minutes alone with something that had no emotions. Likewise, Henry had welcomed the opportunity to be alone with only his own thoughts.

"What's troubling you?" Jim's mother seemed to think better of her question and rephrased it. "I mean, what's troubling you the most?"

Henry fidgeted in his seat. He might as well tell her the truth. She'd sense it if he tried to hide it, anyway. "I guess it's that my parents lied to me all these years. It's bad enough to find out you're a freak, but to find out your mother did it to you is, well . . ."

Henry stopped and felt his face turn red. What he had said applied to Mrs. Forbes and Jim as much as it did to himself and his mother. He struggled to find a way to apologize.

"Don't worry, Henry. I had to deal with all this years ago." Her eyes glistened in the afternoon light. "We all did. Your mother didn't force any of us. We *wanted* to be part of her experiment. We weren't trying to turn you kids into freaks. We wanted to give you something special."

"Special isn't always good." Henry kept his voice level, but his heart thumped out his anger.

"No, it isn't." Mrs. Forbes wiped a tear from her cheek. "Henry, you know I feel what you feel, but I'll try to explain this in a way that will help *you* feel what we felt then, what we feel now."

"Huh?" Henry jiggled his head, trying to make sense of her confusing speech. She laughed at his reaction as she patted away another tear. "Will you listen?"

He didn't know if the tears she shed were in response to her own emotions or his, but he nodded his head. It wouldn't hurt to hear her out.

"Did your mother explain what she did for us?"

"She used some scientific words I didn't understand. I know she altered your genetics and hoped it would be passed down to your kids." The venom in his words surprised Henry.

"She cloned molecules from each mother. Then she used an enzyme to cut out certain genes and replace them with altered genes to form recombinant, or recombined, DNA that she injected into our bodies." She sat taller and made a fist. "We felt we were part of a momentous step in the evolution of humanity."

"But she messed around with us, too, and we weren't even born yet." Henry took deep breaths, trying to control his anger for Mrs. Forbes' sake.

"When you *were* born, it changed your mother. I took Jim with me to visit you both in the hospital. I'd had two months with Jim, and I suspected she'd need someone to talk to." She looked at Henry as if to make sure he was listening.

After Henry nodded, and she continued. "We sat there, holding the two of you. I remember how tenderly your mother looked at you. She said, 'What have I done?' over and over. She hugged you and said, 'I can't let them study him. He's not an experiment. He's my Henry.'"

Tears formed in Henry's eyes, and he could see that Mrs. Forbes sensed his change by her softened tone. "She waited until the last of the babies was born, and then she told the group how she felt. Everyone agreed." Mrs. Forbes smiled at Henry. "When it was theoretical, it all sounded grand, but when you kids were born, it became very personal. Your mother has paid an immense price for what she did." Her lips quavered, and she bit them for a moment. "We all have."

Henry lowered his head. "They told me about the babies who died. How could those parents forgive her?"

"That's the point I'm trying to make. We all knew the risks. We felt the possibilities outweighed them. We thought we were helping form a generation of superior humans. Think of the good you can do with your abilities."

Chuck's terrorist activities came to mind. "Think of the bad we could do."

"We've been concerned about that, too. That's why we meet four times a year. Your mother has done her best to help us raise our children to be good, productive citizens."

Henry snorted. "It didn't work with Chuck."

"You see, that's one of the problems. Mrs. Messer truly believes Chuck is a wonderful boy. We've tried to explain to her that he's good at home because she puts good thoughts in his head. She won't believe he's different when she isn't with him."

Henry gave her a crooked half smile.

A whiny voice interrupted them. "What I don't understand is why you picked this stupid empathic thing for me." Henry's eyes shifted to a spot over Mrs. Forbes's shoulder and focused on Jim's brooding face.

"Oh." Mrs. Forbes startled at Jim's voice and then moved her feet to let him into the room.

Jim plopped down in the chair. Now that he got a close look, Henry saw that Jim's eyes were leaking, too.

Mrs. Forbes laid a hand on her son's shoulder. "I didn't pick it. Trish had to use what we were already good at as a starting point. It would have been easier on you if you'd been a girl."

"*Thanks*, Mom. That makes me feel *so* much better."

Mrs. Forbes tousled her son's hair. "Once you get used to it, you'll find it's not so bad. You may not be able to leap tall buildings, but you'll know who you can trust. That will save you a lot of heartache . . . and money."

84

Grinning at his mother, Jim wiped his eyes. Watching them, Henry realized he missed his own mother more than he'd known. More than his anger, more than feeling betrayed, he wanted to see her again.

Chapter 17

As Henry and Jim emerged from the main building the next day before school, Oscar ran up to them. He all but danced around the playground. "You were right. I can do it."

The boy obviously hadn't thought through all the issues. Henry's talk with Jim's mom last night had helped, but being a Tweak still disturbed him.

Jim smiled a welcome. "Let's move out of the way, so no one can hear."

The three boys clustered near the dumpster, out of sight of most of the others.

Oscar took a deep breath and started in. "I didn't like what Mom cooked for dinner last night, so I thought, 'I need time. I need time,' over and over again. The whole family kept looking at their watches. It seemed to take forever to eat that awful stuff."

It didn't make sense for Oscar to torture himself. Henry asked, "Why didn't you make it go quickly?"

"Because that's what I would usually do, and it would seem normal to me. This way, it proved I can do it. I can slow down time. That means I can help you put Chuck in his place."

Jim slapped Oscar on the back. "You're a born scientist, boy."

Oscar grinned at him. "That's not all I did, though. I made time go faster while my sister talked on the phone and slower while she did the dishes! Boy, was that fun."

"That's the spirit." Henry started to catch Oscar's enthusiasm. "Now we need to come up with a way to defeat Chuckles."

Jim barked out orders like a drill sergeant. "Let's find the girls. Henry, find Tina. We'll find Shandra." He looked at his watch. "We can talk in the fifth-grade room until it's time for school to start."

Henry saluted and spat back, "Yes, sir." He didn't want to delay now that they had completed the recruitment phase of the project.

By the time Henry led Tina into the fifth grade room, Shandra had arrived and explained to her teacher that the five of them were drawing up a proposal for a new school club. The teacher offered them the back table for their discussion and left them alone.

Tina reported she had practiced all evening until she could get a premonition on cue. "Usually, I can tell what's going to happen for the next half hour to an hour, and I'm getting more definite images every time I try it."

Shandra took notes again. "I want to be clear on how each of our abilities can be used. So, you should be able to warn us if things are getting out of hand?"

"Yeah, as long as I know who to concentrate on," Tina said, "I can tell what's going to happen to them." She cocked her head and then giggled. "No wonder my mother always knew when to nag me about wearing a coat or studying for a test."

She needed to make sense of her new view on life, but they still had a lot to do. Henry pointed at the clock. "There's only ten minutes left before school. We need a battle plan."

Shandra scribbled out their plans as they brainstormed ideas, scratching out previous suggestions as better alternatives developed. They had enough time, thanks to Oscar, and everyone agreed to the final scheme as the bell sounded.

Henry gave them last minute instructions. "We'll practice at recess. Meet at the backstop out on the grass after you eat. And, Oscar, don't dawdle at lunch. Get us all out of there quickly."

* * *

At recess, Mr. Goetz surveyed the boys playing soccer or wall ball and the girls jumping rope or hitting the tetherball. Then he noticed five students out on the baseball field walking around and talking to each other.

To everyone else, it looked as though they were acting out some make-believe scenario. To Mr. Goetz, any activity that included four of the five people on his list held great interest. He moseyed around the blacktop and grassy area, careful not to pay too much attention to the baseball diamond.

During his rounds, he noticed Shandra directing the action from a small pad of paper she tucked in her pocket when not in use. She placed Oscar out in front of the backstop and hid Henry and Jim behind it. She and Tina took up posts farther away. When all had given a thumbs-up, Oscar pretended to talk to someone in front of him as the others watched. Then they all jumped around and yelled a lot. Whatever they had in mind, he suspected he'd found the last of the children he'd come to investigate.

* * *

The Tweaks gathered around the backstop one last time.

Shandra said, "Okay, I think we're ready."

"Yep." Henry nodded. "You can stop slowing down time now, Oscar." He looked across the field and noticed Mr. Goetz heading their way. "Quick! Think of something to tell him we've been doing."

Shandra shouted, "If you boys won't teach us those karate moves, then we won't play with you anymore. Come on, Tina."

With that, the two girls stomped off past Mr. Goetz.

The teacher stopped in front of the three boys. "Hi Jim, Henry, who's your friend?"

Henry peered up at his teacher. "This is Oscar. He's in the fifth grade."

"Oscar, huh?" The teacher gave the boy a warm smile. "What's your last name?"

Oscar swallowed hard and answered, "Newell," in a small voice.

Henry tried to read his teacher's thoughts, but he only picked up Oscar's name repeated over and over again. Mr. Goetz acknowledged Oscar with a nod and sauntered back in the direction of the blacktop.

That was weird. Henry looked first at Oscar and then at Jim. "What was that all about?"

Jim shook his head. "I don't know, but he sure seemed excited to meet Oscar." Jim turned to the younger boy. "Not that anyone wouldn't want to meet you, Oscar, but he acted *way* too interested."

Chapter 18

According to plan, the five Tweaks met beside the dumpster after school. Henry probed each face and each mind to assure himself they were ready. He relaxed when he discovered that, after practicing so much, even Oscar seemed confident in their plan.

Shandra took out her notes. "Okay, Tina, concentrate on Chuck. What's he going to be doing for the next half hour?"

Tina scrunched her eyes shut. Henry noticed the revulsion on her face as she viewed Chuck's after school shenanigans. "He's with Bruce chasing a cat." Tina winced a moment later, and Henry wondered what horror was about to befall the cat.

Shuddering, Tina kept her eyes closed. "That cat's tail will never be the same." She dipped and raised her head as if following the action, and her short, straight hair bounced around her face. Finally, she opened her eyes. "I've got it. They'll be at the little corner store on the next block in a while. I saw Oscar there with them, but I don't know how it turns out." She shot Oscar a worried look.

Oscar shrugged his shoulders as if he understood, but Henry picked up a kernel of doubt in his thoughts.

Not wanting Oscar to think about it and back out, Henry said, "Let's go," and headed across the playground toward the sidewalk. Oscar and the others followed him, but Henry noticed Jim hung back for a moment, looking around the playground before shrugging and running to catch up.

They hurried down the sidewalk to the far corner of the next block. Henry and Jim crouched behind the overflowing garbage cans at the near side of the store while the girls crossed in front of the brick building. Shandra found a bush to hide behind at the far corner, and Tina slid in back of a maple tree that bordered the yard next door. Oscar stationed himself by the ice machine in front as planned. Henry squelched a laugh at Oscar's attempts to "act casual."

Jim didn't seem to share Henry's enjoyment of the scene. "Oscar, quit slowing down time. Speed things up, already. You're the bait, Dude. Now start bobbing."

"Shh!" Shandra's voice floated to them from behind her bush.

Oscar took a deep breath. Henry nodded to Jim to indicate Oscar had started thinking he couldn't wait for Chuckles and Bruiser to get there despite his obvious desires to the contrary.

Henry peeked around a slimy garbage can then ducked back. The two hooligans had rounded the corner down the block and were headed toward them. Oscar took slow steps as if intending to enter the store.

It was obvious by Oscar's fidgeting that the kid wanted this to be over quickly. Henry gained a new respect for the slender boy in glasses when he heard him think, *I need more time*. They had agreed to start the proceedings in slow motion then speed things up when Chuck got confused. Henry wondered now if Oscar would follow the plan when he came face to face with the two bigger boys.

Chuck stomped up to the front of the store and stopped in front of Oscar. "Hey, here's an easy mark." Chuck indicated Oscar with his thumb. "Lighten his pockets for him."

Bruce stepped forward, but Oscar held his ground, shaking only slightly. Henry shifted to get a better view and noticed several scratches on Bruce's hands. That cat's tail may be damaged, but its claws were evidently fine.

Stepping close, Bruce towered over the younger boy. "Hey there, pipsqueak, you'd rather buy my friend and me a candy bar than lose those glasses of yours. Wouldn't ya?"

Before Oscar could respond, Henry and Jim stepped out from around the building to his right, and the girls appeared behind Chuck, completing the trap.

Bruce turned to Chuck. "What's going on?"

Ignoring him, Chuck made a fist and scowled at Henry. "What are you peons doing?"

"We'd like to have a talk with you." Henry stepped between the two bullies and Oscar just as the boy and Tina yelped in unison, "We need to get out of here."

Henry shook his head. "He's making you think that. Stick with the plan."

Bruce glared at Henry. "What are you talking about? Chuck can't make them think anything."

The one thing they hadn't completely figured out was how to get rid of Bruce without letting him know they had special abilities. Henry decided to try a straight forward approach.

He mustered his most sarcastic tone. "I meant he made them want to run away because he's so big and powerful." He leaned closer to Bruce. "You don't *really* want to do the stuff he makes you do." Henry's tone softened. "Do you, Bruce?"

The larger boy stared at Henry, and his mouth dropped open as if he'd never thought about it before. Everyone, even Chuck, stood facing Bruce, waiting for his answer. His mental gears seemed to be turning in slow motion. Bruce shut his mouth, opened it again, and then shut it once more.

Chuck seemed fed up. "Well, do you?"

His one friend studied the bully as though he had never seen him before. "No. Not really."

Glaring at him, Chuck demanded, "Wha'dya mean? We're a team."

Bruce shut his eyes for so long Henry began to wonder if he'd fallen asleep. Finally, Bruce tilted his head one way then the other. Then he opened his eyes and spoke. "I always think it's the best thing to do when I'm with you, but later, I don't know why I did it."

Shandra jumped on the opportunity. "Why don't you go home and think about what *you* want to do."

"Uh." Bruce looked at Chuck and wrinkled his forehead.

Chuck returned the stare with raised eyebrows. "Well, are you going to run out on me?"

Whatever happened next, Henry didn't want to be too close to the two meanest kids in school. Henry took a step back.

Chuck snorted as Bruce shrugged and then started walking down the sidewalk.

Before Chuck could call after him, Shandra squinted and stared at the bully's sweatshirt. The fabric wiggled and twisted. Chuck grabbed the ribbed bottom edge on both sides. Shandra bent toward him and hunched her shoulders.

Chuck's arms shot into the air, bringing the bottom of his sweatshirt over his head and engulfing him in darkness. His hands flailed, but his arms seemed pinned tight against his head.

The plan was working. Henry smiled.

Chuck yelled, "Get this off me!"

After a few seconds, Henry shot Jim a question with his eyes.

Jim paused with his head cocked. "Yep, he's scared enough."

The two boys grabbed Chuck's shirt hem and pulled it down while Shandra started the speech she'd been practicing all afternoon.

"It's only your sweatshirt, Chuckles. Are you afraid of your own shirt? You're not so big and powerful, after all. Are you?" She paused as Chuck blinked and focused on her. Then she went on. "Here we've all been thinking you were so brave, but you're exactly like everyone else."

"No, I'm not. I'm better than everyone else." Chuck seemed to have regained his composure, and he stated it as a fact, not opinion.

Tina stretched to her full height. "What makes you better?"

It was Chuck's turn for introspection. Obviously, he had never thought about a reason for his assumed superiority any more than Bruce had thought about why he did what Chuck wanted.

Finally, the bully tried to put his one conviction into words. "I, . . . I . . . I just am."

Stepping toward him, Shandra reached out her hand. "Chuck, *we* know why you're special. The thing is, you aren't the only one, and it doesn't give you the right to boss other people around."

Chuck took a step backward. "What are you talking about?"

It was Jim who answered. "You do have one thing that makes you different from everyone else. The reason Bruce always does what you want is that you put ideas in his head."

Chuck shook his head. "Principal Smothers always says that, too, but Bruce thinks like I do."

"No." Jim tried again. "I mean you actually put the thoughts into Bruce's mind. Think about it, Chuck. Did Bruce *ever* come up with a plan you hadn't already thought of?"

Chuck stared into space as he thought. "He, um, he wanted to . . . No, that was my idea." Oscar's face showed the concentration it took to slow time down to give Chuck a chance to think. They had agreed not to let him go home to his mother before he came to grips with his new reality.

Jim repeated the question. "Did Bruce ever *once* come up with a scheme on his own?"

"Well." Chuck shook his head again and answered in a deflated voice. "No."

It was time for the final blow. Henry drew closer. "You get it from your mother. She puts thoughts in *your* head, too. That's why you've always thought you were special. Your mother thinks you're special, and she's been putting that idea into your head since you were born."

Chuck took a step back. "How can that be?"

Henry recognized the look in the bigger boy's eyes. He was starting to believe. "Your mother's DNA was tweaked before you were born. You're a Tweak, like us."

Chuck stared up at the store sign. He scratched the back of his neck and mumbled, "That's why I always want what she makes for breakfast." His eyes grew round. "That's why I can't argue with her." He seemed to come back to the present as his voice grew louder. "That's why my parents never fight."

Oscar took a deep breath and delivered his speech. "All of our mothers have a gift, and they passed them down to us." Oscar's chest expanded, and his voice became stronger as he spoke. "You're not the only one who can do something amazing, Chuck, and we're not going to let you push anyone around, ever again." Oscar grinned as he stood up to the school bully.

"I don't believe you." Chuck spat the words at the younger boy. "You're a bunch of nobodies. What could you possibly do?"

"I can manipulate time. Look down the sidewalk." Oscar pointed in the direction Bruce had taken.

Swiveling his head, Chuck obeyed. Bruce was crossing the street at the end of the block. "That can't be. It's been a long time since he left."

Oscar laughed at him. "No, I slowed time down for us, so we could have this little chat without being interrupted."

"That's right." Shandra joined in. "And I pulled your shirt and arms up over your head with my mind."

Chuck laughed. "Sure, you did."

Shandra turned her nose up at him and then scrunched her eyes. The hood of his sweatshirt flopped up and down and then flipped up over his head. Chuck shoved the hood back off his head, wide-eyed and speechless.

Henry took advantage of his stupor. "I read your thoughts. That's how I knew you wanted us to go away."

Chuck's face reflected his confusion. He looked at Tina. "What about you?"

"I can tell what's going to happen. I knew you'd be here." Suddenly, Tina's face registered panic. "Henry, Mr. Goetz—"

"That's right Tina." Mr. Goetz cut her short as he stepped out from behind a tree. "I've been here the whole time." His long arms shot out, and he grabbed Henry and Chuck by the shoulders. "Now I've got you all."

Chapter 19

The other four kids whirled around to face Mr.
Goetz, who held onto Chuck and Henry. They stopped,
frozen. Shandra scowled. "Let go of them."

Mr. Goetz's eyes darted up and down the street. He
released the boys but shifted his position to pin the
group in alongside the ice machine. He smirked.
"Thanks for filling in the blanks for me. I hadn't
figured out what Oscar and Tina could do."

Tina looked from Henry to Shandra. "I'm sorry! I
wasn't thinking about the future."

"It's okay." Four voices assured her at once. Henry
didn't need Jim's emotional connection to understand
Tina's despair.

Mr. Goetz glanced down the street again. "Let's
move this meeting into my classroom and away from
prying eyes." He seemed to think they would obey out
of habit.

"No." Henry stepped in front of the others. "We're
not going anywhere with you, and I don't trust you no
matter how many times I hear you think about not
hurting us."

Mr. Goetz turned to Tina. "Look into the future and see what happens."

She gazed into the distance for a moment. "I can only see the next little while, but I do see us leaving the school safely."

"Well?" Mr. Goetz lifted his hands, palms up, and shrugged his shoulders. "None of us want anyone else to hear this. Would your parents want others to know?"

"No." Henry took a silent poll of his friends' faces. "Okay, if Tina says it's all right, we'll come with you."

Chuck opened his mouth, but Henry said, "Chuck, for once in your life, do what someone else tells you to do."

"Besides," Jim added, "you're confused. This is the only way you're gonna get the answers you want."

Shandra stepped right up to Chuck, peering into his face. "And don't bother trying to put thoughts in our minds. We'd all know it was you."

Chuck shrugged and shuffled after the others with sagging shoulders.

Once inside and seated at the back table, no one took the lead. Henry tried to read Mr. Goetz's mind but found a jumble of thoughts interrupted by fragments of ideas from Chuck who was evidently trying to learn to control his newfound ability. The look of concentration on Jim's face showed he was as overwhelmed with everyone's emotions as Henry was with their thoughts.

Sticking her chin in the air, Shandra spoke for the group. "Mr. Goetz, we're not going to the Institute."

Mr. Goetz pounded the table. "You *do* know about the Institute. Have you been there?"

Henry thought of his mother and father. If Mr. Goetz worked for the Institute, telling him what they knew could put his parents in greater danger. "We won't answer any questions until you tell us who you are."

"I'm your teacher, Henry."

"That's not all you are." Henry glared at him. "You knew there were kids in this school with unusual talents before we did. You've been spying on us to find out more."

Stiffening, Mr. Goetz returned his gaze. Henry zeroed in on his teacher's thoughts and got one clear message. *I'm going to have to trust them.*

Mr. Goetz relaxed. "I'm not with the Institute. I came here to find out if *you* were working for them."

Henry turned to Jim. "What do you think?"

"He's telling the truth. He's afraid and worried."

That seemed to startle Chuck out of a stupor. "So that's your power. No wonder you didn't brag about it like the others." His voice took on a singsong quality. "Jimmy can tell what you're feeling. How cute."

"I know you're scared spitless," Jim shot back at him.

Chuck sank down in his seat and sulked. Henry hoped he'd keep quiet while they worked through this problem with Mr. Goetz. They'd handle Chuck later.

102

Right now, they needed to find out if the teacher was friend or foe. "Okay, Mr. Goetz, but remember," Henry warned, "we know what you're thinking and what you're feeling, so you might as well be honest with us." He couldn't believe he was talking to an adult this way, let alone his teacher. "We didn't know anything about the Institute until this week when my mother told me they funded some work she did. Now you tell us what you know about it."

Mr. Goetz took a deep breath. "It was *your mother*?" He shook his head. "I knew about the experiment, but not who conducted it or which kids had abilities. That's what I came here to learn."

Henry's heart sank. He'd let slip his mother was the scientist. He'd have to be more careful.

The teacher picked up a clipboard and showed them his list. "I never suspected one of the mothers invented the procedure." He fixed his eyes on Henry. "Did she tell you there were twelve women involved?"

The image of his mother, lost in sorrow over those other babies, floated into Henry's mind. "Yes. She told me what happened to the others." He sighed. "Some of the children died, and their families moved away."

Mr. Goetz nodded. "Did she tell you one of them drowned in the river?"

Henry had to think for a moment. His mother had told him so much. "Yes, she said a little girl drowned. She would have had an ability."

"Her name was Karen Hertz, and she was my sister. I went to school right here at Riverton Elementary." Mr.Goetz swung out his arm to take in the whole school. "We changed our last name when we left here. I didn't know why or that my little sister had been part of an experiment." Mr. Goetz paused, a faraway look in his eyes. "Later, I found out my parents were terrified the Institute would come after us."

Their teacher's eyes roved from face to face. He seemed to be gauging the reaction of his audience. Henry tried not to show the panic and confusion swirling inside him.

Finally, taking a deep breath, Henry asked the question he was sure was on every Tweak's mind. "*Did* the Institute try to find you?"

Mr. Goetz shifted in his chair. "Not that I know of. My parents were killed in a car accident two years ago right after I finished college. At least I *thought* it was an accident until their lawyer gave me a sealed envelope." He paused, blinked back tears, and swallowed. "My mother left me a long letter explaining about the experiment and the Institute. Then I started wondering if the Institute or the other people in the experiment had killed my parents to make sure they didn't talk."

His harsh tone grated on Henry, but Shandra hurried to reassure the teacher. "None of our parents were involved. They're as afraid of the Institute as your parents were."

Henry leaned forward. "That's right. My mother went there today to try to convince them her experiment failed." His voice cracked and so did something deep inside him, releasing emotions he'd kept buried all week. He took a deep breath. "None of our parents want us to have to go there and be tested, not even my mother."

The doubts that had plagued him fled, and the truth of his words settled in their place. If only he could tell his mother he believed her, trusted her. Henry pretended to look out the window, struggling not to cry in front of Shandra again. He bumped his knee against Jim's under the table.

Jim gave him a not so gentle shake. "Yeah, Henry's mommy loves him *sooo* much. She couldn't stand to send him off to the big bad Institute to perform tricks for the mad scientists."

The Tweaks all laughed. Henry beamed his thanks to Jim as he mussed his blond curls in fake reprisal.

Mr. Goetz spoke over their noise. "Look, kids, this isn't funny. I've spent most of the last two years researching the Institute for Genetic Improvement. They are deadly serious. Some of the things I've learned are frightening."

He walked over to his desk and brought back a folder. Opening it, he passed around newspaper clippings and Internet printouts. He held up a computer flash drive. "I have a video of a scientist claiming they are developing physically enhanced soldiers for the military. It's possible there are other kids out there who've been genetically engineered to be extremely strong and agile. It's rumored bad things happen to anyone who crosses Dr. Braun and Dr. Grey."

Oscar raised his head, pushing his glassed up on his nose. "Who are they?"

Mr. Goetz retrieved a newspaper clipping from Tina and held it up for them all to see. "Dr. Cameron Braun is the head of the Physical Applications division, and Dr. Nigel Grey is the head of the Mental Applications division. Your experiment would be under Dr. Grey's department."

He pointed at a picture of a short, balding man in a lab coat. "He's a brilliant scientist, but he's also cold and calculating. He doesn't take no for an answer."

A vague uneasiness plagued Henry. "Why are you so concerned about all this if your sister and parents are gone? It doesn't have anything to do with you."

Mr. Goetz shrugged. "I have my reasons. I had to leave my home and my friends at fourteen and could never talk to them again or even let them know where we moved. Now that my parents aren't in danger, I want to know if it was all necessary."

For several minutes, no one spoke as the children passed the research around the table. They all jumped when a snatch of music blared from Jim's pocket.

He drew his cell phone from his pants as two other ring tones sounded. Jim, Shandra and Chuck looked at their identical text messages. *Call home NOW.*

106

Chapter 20

After several phone calls and more than a few explanations, Henry and the other Tweaks sat in the Powell's ample living room, waiting for the other parents to arrive. Except, of course, Henry's parents wouldn't be coming. This first joint meeting of the Tweaks and the Riverton Book Club had been hastily convened to discuss developments concerning Henry's parents, and he itched to get started.

As each set of parents arrived and huddled with their child, Henry noticed his teacher seemed to grow more nervous, fidgeting in his seat and gazing at the newcomers in a way that reminded Henry of a cornered animal. Henry knew Mr. Goetz had decided to trust the Tweaks only an hour ago, but would that trust extend to their parents?

Henry closed his eyes to block out the others scattered around the room and concentrated on Mr. Goetz's thoughts. *My parents lost faith in these people. Can I confide in them? Will they accept me? Here it comes.*

When Henry opened his eyes, Mr. Goetz stood as Shandra's mother crossed the room and offered her daughter's math teacher her hand. "We were heartbroken when little Karen drowned." When Mr. Goetz placed his hand in hers, she patted it. "And we're equally sorry to hear your dear parents are gone, too. At least you've come back home."

Her husband cleared his throat. "I don't mean to seem uncaring, but we need to discuss the matter at hand immediately."

"Of course." Mr. Goetz loosened his Spiderman tie. "I feel a bit out of the loop, and I'm sure you're reluctant to have me here, but . . ."

"Nonsense." Shandra's father placed his hand on Mr. Goetz's shoulder. "If it hadn't been for poor Karen's accident, she and your parents would be sitting here. We all agree. If you want to take their place, you're welcome."

Jim's mother joined the conversation but never left her son's side. "Mr. Goetz, Jim has told me what you said at school this afternoon. We're sorry your parents didn't trust us."

She leaned toward him. "If they had stayed here, they would have known we've spent the last twelve years dreading this day. Henry's parents have driven into the city to try to convince Dr. Grey at the Institute that the experiment failed." She put her arm around Jim, and Henry, sitting in a chair next to them, felt completely alone for the first time in his life.

Jim's mother twisted in her seat and scrutinized Henry for a moment. "I know you love your parents." A smile lit her eyes but vanished when she spoke again. "You're worried, as we all are, about them. We got a call from your dad a couple of hours ago. Your mom went to the Institute this morning and had not returned. He called her, but she didn't answer her cell phone."

Concern etched wrinkles in her face. "The receptionist who answered his call to the Institute told your dad that Dr. Patricia Lang had never arrived. He headed over there to see what he could find out."

Before Henry could respond, Chuck jumped up. "That creepy Dr. Grey kidnapped her, maybe both of them. Let's charge in there. With our powers, they wouldn't stand a chance."

Mrs. Messer grabbed her son's arm and pulled him back down beside her on the couch. "No. I don't want you anywhere near that place."

Shandra's mother's voice was much calmer. "Your mother's right, Charles. We don't know what's happened. We need to wait and see what Henry's father found out." She patted Henry's shoulders as if it would soften the blow. "He promised to call back by four o'clock. Let's give him another hour."

It was almost five. Henry took a deep breath and reviewed the multiplication tables to block out the panicked thoughts that swirled through the minds of his friends.

Chapter 21

While the Tweaks plotted their confrontation with Chuck earlier in the day, Henry's mother sat in an opulent office across a highly polished desk from Dr. Nigel Grey, head of Intellectual Applications of the Institute for Genetic Improvement. Trish Johnson had two missions. First, but not foremost, she needed to convince Dr. Grey her experiment had not succeeded.

Second, and most important, she had to give this brilliant scientist no clue the test subjects included her son. The Institute had a reputation for getting what it wanted. She had heard rumors over the years that some of their methods were subversive, even bordering on being cruel.

Dr. Grey adjusted his glasses and put a pleasant expression on his round face. "After funding your research, you can imagine our disappointment in your last report." He smoothed the few hairs he'd combed over his bald head. "We expected to have results by now."

Trish arranged her features to display a concern and regret she did not feel. "Believe me, I share your disappointment. The experiment seems to be a complete failure. None of the children show any signs of being gifted."

Dr. Grey squinted as he framed his question. "What of the mothers?"

Using her best clinical tone, she delivered the speech she had practiced on the drive into the city. "Early results were encouraging, but their abilities never developed much beyond normal ranges. For example, Mother E has more sympathy for others than the average person but not in the range of an empath."

"I see." Dr. Grey's tone did not match his words. Trish concentrated all her energy on him and confirmed that he thought she was holding out on him. He cleared his throat and continued. "There were seven promising children; I believe?

"Yes, out of the twelve test subjects, seven children were born with the green eye marker. One died in an accident at a young age. I have been monitoring the remaining six children, and, as I said, there are no indications any of the children have inherited an extraordinary ability. I meet with the six women four times a year. I also meet with the two mothers whose children did not have the control marker once a year. They and their children test well within normal ranges.

After referring to some papers on his desk, Dr. Grey intensified his attack. "Our contract states if we provided medical care for the pregnancies and your expenses, the progeny would be presented for testing as they entered adolescence." His words stopped there, but

Trish could hear his thoughts clearly. *We should have insisted on testing the mothers, too. Ah, well, we'll be able to get them after we have their children.*

The effort of reading his mind weakened Trish, and she adjusted herself in her straight-backed chair. She reminded herself to act calm and detached, like a scientist, not a mother.

She tried to keep her voice even. "We agreed those who developed abilities would be made available to you. There are none."

His voice sounded strained. "We'd like to determine that for ourselves."

Trying to turn her fear and exhaustion into outrage, Trish allowed her voice to rise in volume and lower in pitch. "It was *my* experiment. I was to have complete control."

"It was *our* money." Dr. Grey cocked his head toward her, lending emphasis to his words.

Recognizing her cue, she got a check out of her purse and handed it across the desk. "The families of the six children asked me to return the money they received from you since the experiment failed. Here is my personal check for the medical expenses of the six women I've been tracking along with a substantial part of the money that—"

"We don't want the money back! We want the test subjects as promised. Give me their names and addresses, and we will collect our, uh, the children."

112

Trish sat taller and squared her shoulders. "I can't do that." She tried to read his thoughts, but she could only zero in on a few words. "*Can't leave . . . force her . . . sodium pentothal . . .*"

Dr. Grey dropped all pretenses at civility. "You are in breach of our contract. I could have you sued."

Trish felt the ice of his words and his gaze. She glared back at him. "You could," she agreed, "if you want to explain, in court, that you financed semi-legal experiments intended to develop superhuman abilities in children with the intent of locking them up and exploiting them."

As Dr. Grey fidgeted, Trish snatched one of his thoughts. *Threats won't work.* Aloud, he returned to his former cajoling tone. "Now, Dr. Lang, we're both scientists, not lawyers. You don't need to worry. The children will be well cared for. We simply need to evaluate the success of your methods, the feasibility of duplicating your work."

"I have told you," Trish stressed each word, "my methods failed. There is no point in duplicating any of it. You have my reports."

"I'm afraid that's not good enough. Your reports are contradictory and misleading." His eyes hardened, and he gave a slight nod. "Yes, I'm sure a few days of contemplation will encourage you to meet your responsibilities to us."

Dr. Grey reached across his desk to a small box and pushed a button. "You'll be our guest, of course, while you decide."

Before Trish could stand, two men in blue uniforms entered the room and, flanking her chair, each grabbed her by an arm.

"Take her to a guest room in C wing. Her treatment will start tomorrow." Dr. Grey gave a flick of his hand, dismissing the three of them, and Trish was roughly escorted out the door.

Chapter 22

Several hours later, Henry's father entered the Institute for Genetic Improvement. Viewing the sterile white floors and shiny interior, he felt as if he'd entered a giant, translucent space ship. The walls, constructed of triangular glass panels, led the eye upward as if to a bright, new future.

A stainless steel counter with a glass top faced him, and he noticed a young woman in a crisp white lab coat perched there. He approached her, introducing himself as Dr. Lang's husband. "It's important I see my wife immediately." He felt the staccato of his pulse and hoped his voice sounded steadier.

"I'd be glad to take you to your wife, Mr. Lang," the petite receptionist replied. He recognized the voice that had denied seeing Patricia Lang when he'd called an hour earlier.

He followed the young woman to a door marked "C Wing." She inserted a key and twisted it before swinging open the heavy door and moving aside to let him pass. He looked down the empty hall and back at the receptionist. She raised her eyebrows at him then extended her hand, motioning him onward. He walked through the doorway and paused. A series of closed, numbered doors lined both sides of the long corridor. The receptionist gave him a thin smile. "Right this way."

He watched her stride past him and followed her brisk steps until she stopped at the first room on the left. She sorted through the keys on her ring, chose one, and unlocked the door. "This is your wife's room."

Gesturing for him to go in, she backed up to allow him to enter. He peered into the room and saw a figure on the bed turn toward him. As he entered, his wife leapt from the bed and into his arms.

He held her tightly. "Trish, I was so worried."

His wife buried her head in his chest and shuddered. Then she lifted her eyes to his. "We've got to—"

The door slammed shut behind them, and he heard the click of the lock.

Chapter 23

By six o'clock, the fear in the Powell's living room had subdued even Chuck's egotism, and everyone sat in silence, waiting. Henry had spent the last hour shutting his mind off from the thoughts of the others. His own fears for his parents were enough to handle without being drawn into Mrs. Messer's doubts about his mother's loyalty or Oscar's father's plans to take his family and hide out at his aunt's place in Florida. Henry noticed Mrs. Forbes and Jim huddled together on the couch, withdrawn, he assumed, in a similar effort to block the emotions of the group.

Finally, Henry had had enough. "We've got to do something, go there and demand to see my parents. My dad would have called by now if he could."

Oscar adjusted his glasses and cleared his throat. "What if the Institute finds out you're part of the experiment?" He grimaced. "That we all are? We can't walk in there and hand ourselves over to be—"

Tina clicked her tongue. "That's the problem. We don't know *what* they'd do." She squeezed her eyes shut for a moment. "I've been trying, and I can't see that far into the future. All we have to go on are rumors."

Slipping his cell phone into his pocket, Mr. Goetz stood from his wooden chair in the corner. "I'm afraid there's more than that. I've been researching the Institute ever since my parents died." He gazed at the carpet. "I am convinced they will stop at nothing to get what they want."

Jim's mother sat up straighter and roused herself. "Do you have any proof beyond your parents' fears?" She stole a glance at Jim. "Has the Institute done anything to indicate the children are in danger?"

Mr.Goetz tilted his head. "I met with Dr. Grey six months ago. I told him I was writing an article on recombinant DNA for a magazine. At first he seemed very pleasant."

"At first?" Chuck asked.

"I wanted to find out how strongly he believed in altering people genetically. I let it slip my editor wanted the article to focus on the ethical and political issues and dangers of 'playing god' through genetic engineering."

Shandra's eyebrows shot up. "What'd he do?

"He transformed into a completely different person. His nostrils flared, and his jaw tensed. He chose his words carefully, but I left fully convinced he would do anything to protect the Institute."

Henry jumped up. "But did he *do* anything?"

"I don't know all he did, but my friend is a receptionist for the magazine I mentioned. The Institute's lawyer called threatening them with a lawsuit within an hour after I left."

Mr. Goetz's voice took on an ominous tone that gave Henry chills. "A car followed me when I left the Institute and everywhere I went for two days. Then I called Dr. Grey from a restaurant and told him my editor had killed the article. Three minutes later, the car left the parking lot, and I never saw it again."

Regret at the way he'd treated his mother took hold of Henry's heart and shook it like a terrier with a rope. "I don't care what they do to me." His hands clenched into fists. "I can't abandon my parents."

"Of course we won't abandon them." Jim's mother reached out to Henry. "But we need a plan."

Henry sank back into his seat, but the mention of making a plan stirred Chuck into action. He jumped up. "Like I said, with our abilities, we can do anything."

Chuck's father pulled on his son's hand, trying to get him to sit back down. Mr. Messer's voice was pleading. "This is a job for the grownups." Every parent nodded. It was probably the first time since Chuck learned to talk that Mr. Messer had attempted to control his younger son.

As he did in class to get his students' attention, Mr. Goetz stepped to the middle of the room. "I'm afraid the kids have a point. We need to get to the Johnsons without alerting the staff at the Institute. These kids are better equipped for that than any of you parents."

Henry's ragged heart beat faster. Maybe The Goat could convince the adults.

"That's true." Jim's father shook his head. "But they're children. We can't send them into a dangerous situation." He paused, squinted as if concentrating and then said, "No matter how many thoughts to the contrary Chuck puts in our heads."

Jim patted his father on the back. "I *know* how you feel, Dad, but we're Tweaks. We were made for this kind of thing. We'll know what everyone at the Institute is thinking and feeling. We'll even know what's going to happen."

Grinning, Oscar added, "And we can control time."

Shandra glared at the magazines on the coffee table until they scattered onto the floor. "We're kids, but we're talented kids."

Pulling her father up to a standing position, Tina hugged him around his waist. Her shoulder rested against his belt. "Besides, Big Guy, who do you think can sneak around a guarded building better?"

Mr. McCray patted his daughter on the head. "Well, Tiny Tina, you've got a point."

Tina glared up at her father. "Don't call me that."

It seemed best to take the spotlight off Tina. Henry pointed at his teacher with a thumb. "We'll take Mr. Goetz along as a token grownup. Of course, since he's already shown his face around the place, he'll have to stay in the car."

Mr. Goetz cocked his head at Henry with narrowed eyes and pursed lips. "He means they need a driver."

After more arguments and motherly tears, a half an hour later, even Chuck's mother agreed to let the Tweaks and Mr. Goetz mount a rescue. Henry felt relieved to be doing something. Then his teacher dropped a bomb the size of Milwaukee.

"There's one more thing. I promised to wait until I made sure I could confide in all of you." He shifted in his chair. "You've entrusted me with your children's safety. I have to trust you with mine."

Henry looked at his teacher, more puzzled than he'd ever been in math class.

Mr. Goetz stood and faced the group. "Karen's alive. My parents told you she drowned, so no one would try to find us. She's thirteen years old, and she's been with us for most of the last hour."

Chapter 24

Henry fell back in his chair, shocked. "What? Where is she?"

"Alive?"

"Here?"

Shandra's mother's voice rose over the cacophony. "What are you talking about?"

"Settle down, everyone." Mr. Goetz lifted his hands in the air and lowered them. "Karen's ability is astral projection. She can mentally leave her body for short periods and view what's happening somewhere else without being seen." He took his phone from his pocket. "I texted her when we started planning what to do, and she has been here, mentally, off and on since then."

"Geez." Jim looked as if he smelled something rotten. "Why did the girls get the cool abilities?"

Shandra stuck her nose in the air. "Because girls can handle the stress and not try to take over the world."

Mrs. Powell scowled at her daughter but addressed Mr. Goetz. "Where is she, or where is her body, now?"

"She's waiting at my apartment."

Tina's eyes sparkled. "Do we know her?"

"No, she's a little older than the rest of you. She's in seventh grade at the middle school."

Tina's face fell, evidently disappointed at still being, by far, the youngest of the group.

Henry wondered how Shandra felt about the new Tweak, but her face gave him no clue. He resisted reading her mind for about a second, too curious to worry about invading her privacy.

Her passive expression masked the contradicting thoughts he detected in her head. *Excellent, another girl. But does she have to be older than me and have the most amazing ability?*

Henry had heard of the green-eyed monster, but he'd never known it had a turned up nose and auburn curls.

"Well." Shandra's mom broke his concentration. She lightly slapped Mr. Goetz on the arm. "Go get your sister. I'll get some food together, and we'll have a welcome home celebration before we get down to planning the rescue."

Chuck pumped his fist in the air. "It's about time, Mrs. Powell. I've been putting the idea of food into your mind for the last half hour."

She smiled sweetly. "Well, I'm glad to see you're volunteering to help in the kitchen, Charles. You can cut up the salad." Henry almost laughed out loud at the look on Chuck's face. The bully had met his match in Shandra's mom.

Henry watched Shandra's jealousy dissipate twenty minutes later when Karen entered the front door, looked around at the Tweaks, and announced, "Three girls and four boys. *Now* it's even."

Within minutes, the three girls were huddled on a couch discussing hair styles and the latest movies as they ate. Henry caught snippets of their conversation from his spot across the room.

When his food was gone, Henry went to refill his glass from the pitcher on the coffee table. He wasn't really thirsty, but he couldn't read all three girls' minds at once, and he wanted to hear what they were saying.

Karen wiped her napkin across her mouth with a flourish. "That was the best meal I've had in a long time." She eyed her brother. "Mark's idea of a gourmet dinner comes from the frozen food aisle." She looked up at Henry and then back to Shandra. Then she took Shandra's paper plate and stacked it on her own. "Let's take the garbage to the kitchen."

Henry didn't need to read Karen's mind to know he wanted to hear the next part of the conversation. He'd been trying to get close to Shandra for months, and this new girl seemed to have become her best friend in a matter of minutes. What did Shandra find so appealing about this brash newcomer?

As the girls gathered the paper goods from laps and end tables, Henry strolled toward the dining room, hoping to find an eavesdropping spot near the kitchen door. A familiar voice stopped him mid-step.

"Henry?"

"Yeah, Mr. Goetz."

"I'm a little unclear about how your ability works. Let's sit on the couch, and you can satisfy my curiosity."

Henry followed Mr. Goetz to the sofa recently vacated by the girls even though he was more interested in satisfying his own curiosity about what was happening in the next room.

* * *

Shandra led Karen into the kitchen, leaving Tina to put the leftovers on a tray. When the two girls were alone, Karen grabbed Shandra by both shoulders and looked her straight in the eyes. Glancing at the door, she whispered, "My brother made Chuck sound like such a creep." She gave her new friend a gentle shake. "He didn't tell me he was *c-ute* with a capital C."

The blunt honesty and fearless exuberance of the "new girl" excited Shandra. She reached up around Karen's arms to place her hands on the girl's shoulders in a two person huddle. "Don't be fooled. When his mother isn't around, he's a real terrorist in training." She cocked her head. "I never noticed his looks."

"Well, no, you're too busy looking at Henry."

A warmth traveled from the base of Shandra's neck to her hairline. "It shows that much?" She giggled.

"I wish I could read *his* mind. Sometimes I think he likes me, but then he gets quiet and ignores me."

Karen released her new friend. "Yep, he likes you. Ignoring is a sure sign." She shoulder-nudged Shandra then grew serious. "Do you think we can pull off a rescue?"

Shandra shrugged. "I'm not the one who can see into the future. That's Tina."

At that moment, Tina opened the kitchen door, carrying a tray of food. "What's Tina?"

Her voice seemed unusually sharp. They had been the best of friends just a few minutes ago before she and Karen came in the kitchen—without Tina. Shandra took the tray and set it on the counter. "I'm sorry we left you. Karen wanted to talk about Chuck without Henry listening in."

Tina grimaced. "What about Chuck? On our side or not, he's still a bully."

Swinging around to face Tina, Karen sounded offended. "How can you say that? He's the one ready to risk everything to rescue the woman who experimented on our mothers."

Shandra took a step toward Tina. "Karen, you have to remember Chuck's been programmed by his mother to think he's better than everyone. He's been kind of a tyrant at school. It will take a while for us to forget his evil past."

Karen shrugged, but Shandra suspected her new friend would never understand how Tina felt about the boy who had tormented her as long as she could remember—no matter how good looking he'd become.

For a moment longer, Tina glared at Karen then faced Shandra. "So why *did* you say my name?"

Shandra felt relieved to have the tension pass, but Tina's question only revived her original worry. "We were wondering how things are going to work out tomorrow. Can you see it?"

"I've been trying. I can usually 'see' only a half hour or so ahead." Tina seemed to shrink even smaller than usual. "I'd hate to share something I'm not sure about."

Karen rolled her eyes. "Come on. Are we in this together or not?"

Shandra made the "how-could-you-refuse-me?" face that always worked on her father. "Tell us, or we'll imagine even worse all night."

"I don't know for sure." Tina's shoulders sank even lower, but her green eyes met Shandra's. "But I do get an impression of you and Henry shut up in a small, dark room."

Chapter 25

As the sun broke over the distant mountains on Saturday morning, Henry and Jim stood on Jim's front porch, waiting for Mr. Goetz to pick them up.

Henry looked down the road. "What color is Tina's van? Green, isn't it?"

Jim pointed to the corner. "Yeah. That's it now."

The boys piled in the back seat and greeted the others. Henry had tossed and turned all night and felt tired, but most of the others seemed energized and excited about the coming adventure.

Only Chuck complained. "Why do we have to go so early on our day off?"

It seemed to take all of Mr. Goetz's patience to answer in an even tone as he pulled out of the driveway. "Like we agreed last night, we have to do this over the weekend when there are fewer people around."

Chuck waggled his head back and forth. "I know. I know, but why did we have to get up so early?"

Mr. Goetz blew out his breath. "It takes three hours to get to the city, and we need to investigate the facility and make a plan." He nodded toward the middle seat. "Even if Oscar slows down time, it could take most of the day to get ready."

Jim patted Chuck on the back. "Don't worry. Saturday morning cartoons will be on next week, too."

Mr. Goetz eyed them in the rear view mirror. "Okay, we're a team. We have to act like one, or we're going to get into trouble."

"I can handle myself." Chuck laughed. " All I have to do is give the guards the idea to let me go."

The teacher nodded. "You could, Chuck, but they might not act on the idea, and remember, we all know who else is involved."

Chuck tilted his head. "What do you mean? We'll all be there together."

"Think about it." Henry wanted to reach forward and thump Chuck's thick head. Instead, he said, "We aren't the only ones with abilities. We have to protect our mothers."

Mr. Goetz gripped the steering wheel. "If any one of us is questioned, it could be disastrous for all of us." He paused for just a moment. "We're all counting on you, Chuck, especially your mother."

Henry had to make sure Chuck understood. "Dr. Grey doesn't know my mother's married name. He thinks she's Dr. Patricia Lang. He doesn't even know my mother *has* an ability, but he knows the other mothers do. If the Institute can't have the kids, they'll take the mothers."

Tina turned in her seat to face Chuck. "So if any one of us gets caught, we're all in danger. We *have* to watch out for each other."

"Right." Mr. Goetz nodded. "All seven of you need to stick together."

Jim grinned. "We need a battle cry."

Henry thought for a moment and then raised a fist into the air and pumped it with each word. "Tweak 'em!"

The six other kids raised their fists and shouted, "Tweak 'em!"

Mr. Goetz winked at Henry in the mirror. "That's the spirit." Henry picked up the part he didn't say out loud. *Let's hope we can keep it up.*

The drive seemed short, thanks to Oscar, and they found the campus of the Institute for Genetic Improvement without trouble. They spent the first hour and a half driving around the block or parked at the corner, trading cell phone numbers, timing the security guards' rounds, and sketching the general layout of the building.

The one story building consisted of four wings that formed a brick-faced X. A slim glass pyramid topped the lobby and rose above the rest of the building at the center. Henry noticed metal grates lined all the windows. Blinds also covered most of them on the inside, blocking the view from either side.

Each wing ended in a metal door with a small, rectangular window of frosted glass. If the Tweaks kept to the bushes along the brick wings, they should be able to gather information and stay hidden from view.

One by one, the seven spies slipped out of the van and found their way onto various parts of the grounds. Henry, last to leave the vehicle, waited while it pulled over to the curb across the street from the Institute. Mr. Goetz would keep lookout in the van as the others sneaked around behind the shrubbery.

Henry walked toward the building casually then ducked behind the bushes along the front of the parking lot. He crept the length of the greenery until he reached the fence at the far end. He poked his head out. Chuck was making his way around the closest arm of the X-shaped building. At the same time, a security guard came out of the lobby door and stood on the main sidewalk, checking his watch.

If only Henry and Chuck could trade places. Then Chuck could send a message to the guard telling him to go back in and have a cup of coffee since he was early for his rounds. As it was, Henry could only wait and hope.

With a start, he realized he *could* send a message, not to the guard but to Chuck. He flipped open the cell phone Jim's mom had loaned him and texted, *Hide*, to Chuck's phone.

Henry watched Chuck creep further toward the corner then stop and take out his cell phone. The guard ambled along an angled sidewalk toward the spot where Chuck crouched barely out of his sight.

Chuck looked at his phone, and Henry breathed a sigh of relief as Chuck ducked behind a hedge seconds before the guard rounded the corner. Henry felt his own phone vibrate and read Chuck's response. *Thx*

Henry continued along the fence behind a low hedge. When he had cleared the front wing, he dashed across the lawn and dove behind a row of boxwoods that lined the building. He inched his way to the rounded glass block wall of the lobby, searching with his mind for the thoughts of anyone inside.

At first, nothing came to him. Then a shadow passed by the frosted glass, and a string of angry ideas assaulted him.

Doesn't he care that it's Saturday? I should be off to the Daffodil Festival with Derrik. But, no, I have to work because Dr. Grey's latest experiment has gone south—like all the others. I suppose he couldn't wait. Not with the monthly state inspection on Monday.

Henry lost contact with the receptionist as she moved away, so he crept along the wall until he picked up her mental monologue again.

I hope that lady in C wing doesn't have a bad reaction to the drugs like those other people. That one guy looked totally deformed when they took him out of here. At least her husband is with her now.

Henry froze. His parents *were* here, but he was pretty sure Dr. Grey wasn't testing some new drug on them. The injection he gave Henry's parents would

132

probably be some kind of truth serum to make them reveal the identities of the Tweaks.

If only Henry could locate Dr. Grey's office. He needed to get into that weasel's head. He worked his way to the corner of the back wing and came to the end of the hedge. He peeked around the last plant and saw a pad of cement covering the expanse between him and the other side of the wing where the boxwoods continued.

He glanced around. With the coast clear, he stuck his right foot out from his hiding place and pushed off from the building at the same moment the door of the far wing opened.

*   *   *

At the instant Henry darted out from behind the hedge, Chuck heard the door behind him open. He crouched lower between an azalea and the brick wall. If a guard came out and caught that wimpy Henry, he'd recite their names and addresses to the beat of his thumping little heart.

How could he stop the guard for a few seconds to give Henry a chance? Maybe he could get him to look at his watch, but how? Chuck squeezed his eyes shut and sent a thought to the guard twelve feet behind him. *How long 'til lunch?*

He found it hard to concentrate because his own worries kept interrupting. *What if the guard had just looked at his watch? What if he had a weird schedule, and he'd already eaten lunch?* Chuck blocked out his insecurities and sent the message with such force his head started to shake.

When he opened his eyes, Henry was nowhere to be seen. Chuck sank to the ground and peeked around the corner, hoping the guard wouldn't see his movements. The door had only opened a couple of inches since he'd first heard the latch giving way. It swung fully open now, and the guard stepped out. Chuck noticed his left sleeve was pushed up slightly, revealing a watch. It must have worked.

Chuck pulled his head back slowly to avoid drawing the guard's attention as the door closed. Encouraged by his recent success, he sent another message to the guard. *If I unlocked the door now, I wouldn't have to keep unlocking it all day to get back in.*

The guard stepped back toward the door and reached into his pocket. Chuck held his breath. He was going to do it.

Suddenly, the guard shook his head and took his empty hand out of his pocket. Then he walked down the sidewalk leading around the building in the opposite direction from where Henry must be hiding. Chuck counted to fifty then sneaked across the end of the building and dove behind the junipers on the far side, the sharp branches scratching his arms and neck.

He flattened himself against the wall and looked down its length. Almost to the end, he saw Tina, her back to him, hunched in a ball. The little geek must be reading someone's future. There was no way he could slide past her without being shredded by the juniper branches. He'd have to go back the way he'd come.

*   *   *

Tina covered her face with her hands and bent over, so they rested on her knees. She breathed in the pungent scent of juniper and let her mind wander back to her first glimpse of the Institute. A slight young woman had been looking out the main glass door, and Tina focused on her. The vision grew sharper, and as sound joined the picture, she knew it was no longer a memory but a premonition. The image became clear as the receptionist answered the phone.

"You've got to be kidding! I'm stuck here at work, and you ram my car into a minivan?" The receptionist paused, listening to the person on the other end of the call. "I don't care how pretty the daffodils are, Derrik, you should have paid attention to your driving. What am I going to do without a car?"

A noise on the other side of the hedge broke Tina's concentration, and she tilted her head to peer sideways through the prickly shrubs at a pair of black work shoes peeking out from under dark blue pant legs.

A guard stood two feet away on the other side of the bush. She had to get a look at his face to see his future, but if she shifted to look up at him, he'd hear her. She hunkered, frozen in fear, staring at the guard's feet. As much as she wanted to see his immediate future, she didn't want to be part of it. She'd just have to wait for him to leave and hope for another chance.

A sharp thunk sounded a few yards away, and the work shoes moved toward a tree across the lawn. Tina took advantage of the disturbance to face the bush. She watched through the foliage as the burly guard investigated the tree then walked back toward her before angling to his left and continuing down the sidewalk.

Tina breathed a sigh of relief and closed her eyes while his face was fresh in her mind. She could still hear his retreating steps as his future materialized in her mind. She saw him eating lunch at a table in a small room lined with lockers like she'd seen at her mother's gym.

Halfway through his ham sandwich, the guard's walkie talkie squawked, and he stopped chewing to listen.

"Thompson, come to C-1 immediately."

The guard raised the radio to his mouth and pushed a button. "Right away, Dr. Grey."

He shot a longing look at his sandwich and left it.

Tina leaned against the brick wall to steady herself as she envisioned him walking down a hall, across the lobby, and into another wing. He unlocked and entered the first door on the left and closed it behind him.

As the guard looked around the room, the vision got increasingly fuzzy, but Tina recognized Henry's parents. Henry's mom sat on the bed to the left, crying, and Henry's dad, his back to the guard, towered over a short, balding man in a lab coat. "You can't keep us here."

"It's for your safety, really." The man in the lab coat nodded, and the guard twisted Mr. Johnson's hands behind his back. The shorter man pushed a table covered with dishes out of the way and slipped around the two men. He opened the door and ushered them out, following them and snapping the door shut as Tina heard Henry's mom cry out to her husband.

The edges of the vision closed in as the guard strong-armed the struggling Mr. Johnson to the end room on that side of the hall. The last thing Tina saw before she lost the image completely was Mr. Johnson gagged and tied to a chair.

The exertion required to mentally follow the guard for so long took its toll, and Tina sat cross-legged against the building, exhausted. When she heard a noise to her left, she didn't even turn her head. If she was caught, so be it. She didn't have the energy to try to get away.

"Tina, it's me." Shandra's voice revived her, and she looked down the gap between the hedge and the building to see the older girl crawling toward her. "Where's your *friend*?"

Shandra gave her a quizzical look. "Oh, you mean Karen? I don't know." Shandra sat next to Tina with her knees pulled up under her chin. "You're not still mad about last night, are you? I told you I was sorry."

Tina shrugged. Karen was three years older. Of course Shandra preferred her. Anyway, Tina had to admit she liked Karen's lively personality and no-nonsense way of handling the boys. "It's all right. I'm just tired. I've been traveling back and forth in time."

"I know what you mean. I've been trying to work the locks until my head's about to explode."

Tina picked some leaves out of Shandra's curls. "Any luck?"

"No. I don't understand how locks work, so I don't know what to move. I did try to lift the hinge pins on one of the doors. They're rusty, but I think I might be able to get them out. Then we can open the door from the wrong side and get in that way."

"Good." Tina cocked her head and then put a finger to her lips. The crackling of a walkie talkie came to them from down the sidewalk.

*   *   *

Jim backed deeper into the cover of the bushes. He'd been crawling toward the lobby when Tina's fear had grabbed him, pulling him toward her. As he crept

138

closer, he'd seen a guard standing exactly opposite her across the hedge. He'd found a rock in the dirt and threw it at a tree to distract the guard.

When the guard left, Tina had ducked her head, and he'd decided he'd better watch over her in case another guard came along while she did her vision thing. Now, with Shandra there to help her, he could move away and try to find out more about the guards.

Jim crawled along the wall but stopped when he heard the static of the walkie talkie. The guard couldn't be more than a few feet ahead of him out on the sidewalk.

A metallic voice came over the radio. "Be sure to complete your rounds in time to take lunch to the guests in C-1 at noon."

"Roger, out."

The guard moved away, and, try as he might, Jim couldn't pick up a scrap of emotion from him. He continued along toward the front of the building, hoping to "feel" someone more helpful. Instead, he almost bumped into Karen's motionless body stuffed under a scrawny part of the hedge. Jim stopped short and waited for her to come back to herself.

Karen finally moaned and unwound. She looked up at Jim and smiled. "Glad it's you and not a guard."

Jim nodded. "Where have you been?"

"I've been popping in and out of rooms, trying to find someone to spy on. Aside from the guards and the receptionist, the place is practically deserted. I have to keep coming back to make sure my body hasn't been discovered. When I get back, I'm all cramped from lying curled up like this."

Once again, Jim felt compelled to do guard duty instead of accomplishing something productive. Of course, Karen could find out more by combing the inside of the building than he could by crawling around trying to feel unknown people's emotions. "It might help to know there are 'guests' in C-1, wherever that is. Go ahead and search. I'll watch out for you."

"You don't mind? I'm sure it'll be boring."

"You trying to talk me out of it? Get going."

Karen grinned at him and stretched out next to the building before going limp. Great! Karen blocked his path going forward, and the hedge ended a few feet behind him. He couldn't move around at all while he watched over her. A lot of good it did to have a superhero ability if all he got to do was stand guard. No, all he could do was *sit* guard.

Karen's limp body lay perfectly still. She'd better find out something worthwhile.

*   *   *

Karen shut her eyes and willed her consciousness out of her body and upward until her invisible projection floated above the hedge. She gloried in the freedom as she left her body. Below her, Jim squatting next to her still form. With him there, she could be gone

140

as long as she had strength to maintain the projection. Jim would watch out for her and shake her body to bring her back if needed. He couldn't see her wave goodbye to him, but maybe he'd feel her gratitude and trust as she passed through the wall of the building to search for Henry's parents.

She drifted through a door and into the lobby where the petite receptionist sat at a counter, tapping her fingers on the glass top and staring at a clock on the wall. Karen figured Oscar must be doing his job and angled across the lobby to enter another wing.

Finally. A light shone under the first door on the left. Maybe this was C Wing. She entered the room and found herself hovering over a bald man bent over a map of the state. No, this couldn't be the "guest" area. Several diplomas made out to Nigel Grey hung on the walls.

This round little man was the sinister Dr. Grey? Karen would have laughed if she had the use of her mouth. Despite his looks, her brother had warned her about the man. She'd better take him seriously.

As she watched, Dr. Grey picked up an envelope from a pile and checked the postmark. Then he searched the map and drew a star. He repeated the process with each of the envelopes, eventually forming a constellation on the map that enclosed about fifteen towns. He grabbed a piece of paper and jotted down the names of the towns.

Karen checked the return addresses on the envelopes and found that each came from Patricia Lang at a post office box in the city. The postmarks, however, matched the starred names of the towns in the circle. These must be the reports Henry's mother had sent to the Institute through the years.

Dr. Grey drew a vertical line to divide the paper in half with the towns on one side and room to write on the other. Then he stared at the list, tapping his pencil on the desk with increasing speed and force until he threw it down and sorted through the envelopes.

Karen moved to look over his shoulder as he put the postmarks in chronological order and then opened the oldest envelope and took out a paper. When he finished reading it, he stuffed it back and opened the next envelope. He read through the enclosed letter then wrote, "Met parents at preschool," on the empty side of the paper.

He opened each letter and made more notes. When he finished, Karen read the list that included her own fake drowning in a nearby river, the genders of the six other Tweaks, and the abilities Dr. Lang had expected the children to develop.

The little man studied the list for a few minutes then searched on his computer for a list of co-op preschools run by the community college in the area. Going back to his list, he crossed off all but five towns. Karen drew closer and saw Riverton in the middle of the list. She reached for the pencil in an attempt to cross her hometown off the list while he wasn't looking, but in her projected state, her efforts were useless.

She hovered over the little man without paying him any attention for a few moments, thinking through what she'd learned. Finally, it hit her. If they rescued Henry's parents, that wouldn't stop Dr. Grey from finding them.

She snapped out of her reverie when Dr. Grey jumped up and began pacing the room with his hands clasped behind his back. At first, he mumbled under his breath, and Karen couldn't understand his words. Soon, though, his thoughts spilled out in a stream. "Mistake to work with a woman. Too emotional." He stepped over to the desk and ran his finger under the note about meeting the mothers at a preschool.

He resumed his route around the room with a sneer. "Especially mothers. Just can't be objective." He rounded the desk and stopped short, pounding his fist on the map. "That's it! It's not that she bonded with the mothers. She *is* one of them. That explains everything."

He picked up a walkie talkie from the desk and pushed a button. "Get lab C-2 ready. I might need it later today." Then he sat at the desk, rolled up the sleeves of his white lab coat, and opened an email program.

Her energy slipping, Karen struggled to maintain the projection long enough to read the email he'd composed.

General Straung:

I am confident I will have test subjects for your inspection when you visit next month. My government is too narrow-minded to take advantage of this breakthrough, but it is precisely the kind of research your army is interested in buying. I will be retiring and leaving the country after our transaction is complete, so payment must be in untraceable, negotiable bonds.

NG

He centered the cursor over SEND and punched the mouse button. Karen felt her projection begin to dissolve, and she quit fighting the pull of her body as he pounded the desk again. "I am *not* going to let some emotional female keep me from all that money. She'll talk one way or another, and it'll be before the state inspection on Monday."

As Karen drifted through the lobby and toward her body, she glanced out a window and noticed Oscar, face pinched in concentration, huddling beside a dumpster in the parking lot. That goofy little kid should have hidden better.

*   *   *

Oscar shifted his weight to relieve the cramping in his thighs and scooted farther behind the dumpster. It

144

had taken all his concentration to slow time for the others. He hadn't been able to move around or discover anything useful.

He wouldn't have one scrap of information to share when they all got back together. The tingle of his phone vibrating in his pocket startled him and almost made him lose his balance. Looking at the screen, he read the text from Mr.Goetz. *Come back.*

Oscar started to creep out from behind the dumpster, but something caught his eye. A colorful pamphlet about the Institute dangled from under the lid of the garbage container. He pulled it free and stuffed it in his pocket.

*   *   *

Ten minutes later, Henry hoisted himself into the van to find Oscar crammed in the corner of the back seat, slouching and staring out the window. Next to him, Chuck sat sideways, engaged in a whispered conversation with Karen. Tina sat in the shotgun position next to Mr. Goetz, who eyed the rear view mirror with a frown. Shandra scooted over for Henry, and he sat beside her in the middle seat.

Too worried about his parents to be nervous around Shandra, Henry launched in without explanation. "My parents are in there, but I couldn't find them."

The door opened again, and Jim hopped in, sitting with a thump next to Henry. "I hope the rest of you found out more than I did."

Everyone started talking, but Mr. Goetz raised his voice above the others. "Let's find someplace to get lunch and talk. I can't hear all of you at once."

"No." Henry groaned. "We've got to get in there and find my parents. The receptionist—"

Mr. Goetz turned in his seat and silenced Henry with one of his teacher stares. "I know you are anxious, but we'll only get caught if we go charging in without a plan. We need to sit down and go over what everyone learned. Okay?"

Henry opened his mouth to argue, but the logic overcame him, and he nodded.

"All right." Mr.Goetz started the engine. "I saw a pizza place a couple of blocks back. How's that?"

A whoop from Chuck inthe back seat drew everyone's attention. He responded with a shrug. "Well, we'll need our strength for the rescue."

Henry imagined Chuck's mother saying those very words. He turned in his seat to regard the larger boy. The smug look on Chuck's face made Henry suspect he had planted the idea of eating lunch in Mr. Goetz's mind. Henry snorted again and rolled his eyes.

Jim laughed, but Shandra kicked his foot and bunched her eyebrows at him. Then she leaned forward. "That sounds fine, Mr. Goetz. We'll all feel better once we've eaten."

146

Chapter 26

Henry sat with the others at the back of Vencelli's Pizzeria. Mr. Goetz scooted his chair up to the table. "All right, we're going to do this calmly, one at a time." He turned to Oscar on his right. "You first."

The boy frowned. "I had to concentrate on slowing time for the others, but I found this in the garbage." He dug in the pocket of his hoodie and extracted a crumpled tri-folded brochure. It didn't look like it would help much, but Henry kept quiet, not wanting to hurt Oscar's feelings.

Smoothing out the leaflet, Mr. Goetz opened it. "Good work, Oscar. It's a map of the Institute. The four wings are labeled A, B, C, and D." He pointed to a small square. "Here's a grounds keeper's shed in the back. That might be a good place to hide behind."

Oscar pushed his glasses up on his nose, and Henry congratulated him with a rough pat on the back. Maybe this geeky kid had something going for him, after all.

Henry spoke next. "The receptionist mostly ranted about having to work on Saturday. When she finally thought about someone other than herself, I found out my parents are being held in C wing. We've got to get them out."

There was a whine in his voice and Henry appreciated Jim barging in. "I heard on a guard's radio that they're taking lunch to the 'guests' in room one of that wing at noon. That would be half an hour from now."

Jim turned the map, so they could all see it. "Here's C wing. It shows four labs along one side and four guest rooms along the other. Tina, did you find out anything useful?"

The fourth grader looked around at her older accomplices. She turned toward Henry with a little smile. "That receptionist ought to be glad she's at work. Her boyfriend's calling her about now to tell her he smashed her car." After the snickering died down, she addressed the group. "I also saw a guard's future."

She gave Henry a sympathetic look. "He'll be called into a room where your mom is crying, and your dad is yelling at a man in a lab coat, Dr. Grey; I think. The guard takes your dad to another room down the hall and ties him up. I'm sorry."

Henry bit his lower lip. "Do you know when that will happen, Tina?"

"No. I've been practicing, and I can usually see about an hour ahead pretty clearly. If it's further ahead, I don't get much detail. This was really fuzzy, so it shouldn't have happened yet." She looked at Jim on her left. "There were lunch dishes on a table."

Henry tore his paper napkin in half. "We've got to get in there. When the food comes, everyone eat fast.

Except Oscar, you poke at your lunch like you do at school. That will slow our time and help us get back there before anything happens to my parents."

Shandra took a big breath before speaking. "I think I can lift the hinge pins on the outside doors. We might be able to pull a door open from the wrong side and get in that way."

Henry squeezed his chair hard with both hands. *Might be able to get in? Is this the best we can do?* Only Karen and Chuck hadn't spoken. Maybe Karen had found something useful. She had been sitting quietly, resting lightly against Chuck's shoulder through the other reports.

She looked tired, but they didn't have time to rest. Henry said her name, and everyone turned to her.

As Mr.Goetz turned toward his sister, his forehead wrinkled. "Karen, are you all right?"

"I'll be okay. It takes a lot out of me to project for very long, and I really hadn't recovered from last night." She turned to face the group. "I was worried about leaving my body defenseless, so I only projected for a few minutes at a time until Jim came along to protect me."

Turning toward Tina, Karen asked, "Was the man in the lab coat a short, round man with glasses and a moustache?"

Tina nodded. "I only 'saw' his back, but yeah, that's him."

Karen grimaced. "That's Dr. Grey, all right. I saw him in his office with a map. He suspects Dr. Lang is one of the mothers. He told someone to get lab C-2 ready because he might need it later today."

Mr. Goetz looked at Henry, but his question was for his sister. "Do you know what he's planning to do?"

"No, but he gave me the creeps. He's a nasty little man. Karen shifted the map and pointed to the first office in B Wing, right off the lobby. "That's his office, there."

Henry shot Chuck an accusing look. For all his bravado earlier, he hadn't reported doing anything useful all morning. Chuck squared his shoulders. "I looked for a way in, too. I tried to give a guard the idea of unlocking one of the doors. He headed toward it, but then he shook his head and walked off." His shoulders slumped. "I guess he thought better of it."

"Yeah." Jim snorted and leaned toward Henry. "He's probably smarter than Bruiser." After a stern look from their teacher, he tossed a half-hearted apology to his old enemy across the table. "Sorry."

Chuck smirked. "I saved Henry's hide. That guard would have caught him running across the end of the wing if I hadn't made him look at his watch before opening the door."

Touching Chuck's arm Karen beamed up at him. "And those guards have been trained to keep the place locked up. You couldn't undo that with one thought."

Jim shrugged. "Whatever."

Henry bumped his knee against Jim's as Mr. Goetz started another lecture.

"Remember, no matter what your past difference, we have to work as a team now." The teacher glared at Jim as if he'd caught him cheating on a test. Then his voice softened. "You're all new to your abilities. You need to learn what you can and can't do. There'll be some rough spots. You have to be ready to cover for each other."

A waitress, dressed in jeans and a stained apron, brought the pizza at that moment, and they ate it while they made plans. By the end of lunch, everyone knew his or her assignment.

Oscar wiped his glasses on his T-shirt. "I don't know about all this. The guard I saw looked like The Incredible Hulk . . . on steroids."

Chuck stuck out his chest. "Don't worry. We'll give them the Tweakment. They won't know what hit 'em."

Hoping Chuck was right, Henry raised his fist. The others followed suit. "Tweak 'em!"

If all went according to plan, he'd be with his parents very soon. As they left the table, Henry couldn't resist poking into Mr. Goetz's thoughts. He found the teacher still worried about two things—avoiding the guards and keeping his sister away from Chuck Messer.

Chapter 27

After a quick stop to buy some cat burglar odds and ends, Mr. Goetz again deposited the Tweaks at strategic spots around the Institute for Genetic Improvement. Chuck sat next to Karen and watched out the van window as the other Tweaks scurried from bush to hedge to tree around the grounds like hungry ants at a picnic. According to plan, each pair made its way to a designated position.

At the last stop, Chuck hopped out and led Karen across the short space of lawn between B Wing and the groundskeeper's shed in the back of the property. The tiny building would serve as a hiding place while Chuck manipulated the thoughts of the guards and Karen's projection visited the building's interior.

Chuck pointed to the narrow space between the back of the building and the fence. "Can you fit in there?"

"I think so." Karen crawled backward into the gap and lay down.

"Good. You're completely hidden."

"Don't let them find me, Chuck."

"I won't. Don't worry." He lowered his voice almost to a whisper and added, "I won't let anything happen to you."

Karen flashed him a smile so warm it melted his spine, and he stiffened to stay upright. The smile faded from her lips. Her body went limp, and she lay there as still and empty as yesterday's lunch sack.

Chuck knelt down and watched her face for a moment. His hand rose on its own accord and drifted toward a lock of hair that had fallen across her eyes. He tucked the loose curl behind her ear.

Then he stood up and planted a thought in his own brain. *Knock it off, Chuck. Get to work.*

* * *

Crouching in the bushes near a rear entrance to C Wing, Henry began to think that the fourth piece of pizza had been a mistake. His heart raced, and his stomach churned. Somewhere down this hallway, his parents were being held captive, and their freedom rested in the hands of a bunch of kids, including Chuckles and Pokey Ol' Oscar.

"Henry, snap out of it," Shandra whispered, crouching beside him. "I need you to concentrate on listening for a guard with your ears *and* your mind."

"How do you know I'm not?" How could she tell the difference between worry and concentration?

153

"I've watched you enough in math to know when you're distracted."

Her cheeks blushed, and Henry's mind whirled. She'd been watching him as much as he'd been watching her. He couldn't think about that now. He'd file it away for later.

He smiled at Shandra. "Okay, I'm concentrating."

Squinting her eyes, Shandra glared at one of the hinge pins on the door. It jiggled but didn't move. Henry handed her a brand new can of W-D 40.

After squirting some of the liquid on the hinge, Shandra stared at it with renewed intensity. This time, the pin skidded upward half an inch and then stopped with a mouse-sized screech.

Shandra grunted and sprayed the hinge once more. After a quick look at Henry, who nodded encouragement, she tried again. The pin popped up and out of the hinge.

"Whew." Shandra's face had paled, and her breath came in shallow gasps. "That's one. I hope the other one isn't rusted any worse. I don't think I can do much more."

"Do you want to rest?"

"No. There's no time. We have to get in before Mr. Goetz and Jim start their diversion."

She took a deep breath and sprayed the other hinge liberally. It proved to be easier to remove than the first, and she soon held the wrong side of the door open for Henry.

He stuck an arm through the opening, but his shoulder wouldn't fit. "It's not enough. I can't squeeze through." Henry stepped back in defeat. "I'm too big."

Tina's soft voice came from a bush near the entry. "I'm not."

"Give it a try." Henry stepped back. "If you get in, unlock the door for us." Henry cocked his head. Tiny Tina came in handy at the most unexpected times.

Tina stretched herself to her full height, thinning her body as much as possible. She put a leg into the crack and wiggled halfway through. Henry could see her exhale and take another elongating breath. She squirmed and jostled and then popped through into C Wing.

Henry and Shandra replaced the hinge pins and waited. Time crept by. Henry figured Oscar must be nervous and trying to delay starting his part of the plan. At last, the lock clicked, and Tina's head peeked out. "Come on in."

They obeyed and let her out to return to her post before closing the unlocked door behind them.

*   *   *

Creeping to the front of the shed, Chuck peeked out on the empty lawn. He pulled a new pair of miniature binoculars from his jacket pocket and scanned the windows of B Wing. In the office nearest the lobby, the blinds were partway up, and he could make out Dr. Grey's balding head bent over some papers on his desk.

Maybe I can keep him there a while, Chuck thought with a smile. Sending Dr. Grey on a wild goose chase looking for Patricia Lang on the Internet would be today's two-for-one special. It would keep him busy, but he wouldn't find out anything since Henry's mother went by Trish Johnson in Riverton.

To top it off, Chuck planted thoughts about Mapleton being the most likely home of the test subjects in Dr. Grey's mind. If he kept that up, even a scientist would start to think he was onto something.

Karen stirred behind him, and Chuck crawled back to check on her. He found her texting a message. She looked up at him when she finished. "Letting Henry know where his parents are."

He nodded and watched as her body relaxed. Resuming his surveillance post, he tracked along the lobby windows until he came to the entrance of C Wing.

A security guard had one hand on the doorknob. Henry and Shandra should be right on the other side of that door by now. If he could delay the guard, they'd be able to hide.

He shut his eyes and concentrated on the guard. *Tell the receptionist she looks nice today. Tell the receptionist she looks nice today.*

Chuck blew out the breath he hadn't realized he'd been holding as the guard turned and said something to the young woman at the desk. A moment later, the guard went through the door into C Wing and out of sight. Chuck hoped he'd given them enough time. If not, he'd know soon enough.

Chapter 28

Henry and Shandra had made it nearly to the other end of C Wing when he felt his cell phone vibrate. He pulled it out to check the message. "Karen says my dad is in the room nearest the outside door. Mom is still in this last room on the right."

Shandra's face lit up. "She's a good spy. I'm glad she's with us."

"Me, too." Henry gestured behind them. "She also said to hide in the custodian closet back there if we need to."

Henry put his ear to the door of his mother's room then stepped back. "See if you can unlock it with your mind. I'll unlatch the closet door in case we need to get in there in a hurry."

He hurried down the hall and returned to stand guard while Shandra knelt and peered at the doorknob.

After a moment, a sound caught his attention. Henry glanced down the hall to the lobby door. Had the handle moved? He took a few steps closer and cocked his right ear toward the door. Then the lock rattled.

Henry sprinted down the hall, grabbing Shandra's hand as he passed her. Reaching the closet, he pulled the door wide open.

Barreling into the tiny room after him, Shandra closed the door with her mind as the lights in the hall flipped on.

Henry flopped down on an upturned bucket. "Do you think he saw us?"

"Shhh," was the only answer he got.

As they listened, Henry imagined the guard's actions. From the jangle of keys and squeaking hinges, Henry knew he was unlocking and checking each of the labs on this side of the hall. Surely, he wouldn't check the broom closet. Would he?

After two labs, the guard stopped in front of their door. Henry strained to read his thoughts. They were a jumble of music lyrics and baseball scores.

Then one thought stood out that both relieved and terrified Henry. *I'd better finish checking these labs before Old Man Grey decides to move those folks into C2. Too bad they're having such a bad reaction to the drugs he's testing on them.*

Grey had evidently lied to his staff about why he was keeping Henry's parents. He wasn't trying to help them get over a bad reaction to a new drug. He was planning on using a known drug to get information from them.

As the guard moved on, Henry clenched his fists and squeezed his eyes shut, wishing, with every molecule in his mind and body, that Oscar and Tina would start the diversion now.

The guard took a few steps then jingled the keys, and Henry heard the door to what must be C3 open. After a minute, he heard a muffled message on the guard's radio, and then the guard ran back out of the lab.

Shifting to mind reading mode, Henry caught a few words of profanity and the words, *those kids, again*. The footsteps raced down the hall and out the door that Henry and Shandra had sneaked through moments before.

Henry jumped up. "Okay, we can go. He's taken the bait."

After peeking out, Shandra led the way, and Henry followed into the brightly lit hallway.

Even in the empty hall, Henry whispered. "That guard was thinking about Dr. Grey coming soon to take my parents to C2. We need to hurry."

Shandra kneeled down and stared at the doorknob of the first guest room, trying to manipulate the mechanism. "I wish I knew how locks are made."

"You can do it." Henry tried to sound confident, but this part of the plan made him the most uneasy. "If Karen can't find a set of keys, you're our only hope of getting my parents out."

Karen had used a lot of energy last night and this morning, and Henry didn't know how much more she could do. Besides, probably, no one had left keys lying around, and if someone had, they wouldn't be where he could walk up and take them.

He looked up and down the hall. The guard could come back any minute and find the unlocked door. Dr. Grey's office sat in B Wing, fifteen feet across the lobby from where he stood. If he came, they wouldn't be able to hear him until he reached the door to C Wing.

Why had he shut the closet door? They couldn't get back into the small room in time if they had to open the door before jumping in. Unable to decide which direction held the biggest threat, he scanned from one end of the hall to the other.

On his second sweep, a shadow appeared in the frosted glass of the outside door. He held his breath and stared at the window. If the door opened, they'd be caught. The guard would never believe they were neighborhood kids who sneaked in to look around.

What should he do? If he broke Shandra's concentration for no reason, she'd never get the lock opened. He waited, and the shadow passed. Henry took a deep breath as his gaze shifted back toward the lobby door. Halfway down the hall, something caught his eye.

He slipped away to investigate. A moment later, Henry dangled the guard's keys in front of Shandra's face. "Maybe we could use these."

"Where'd you get those?"

Henry tipped his head toward lab C3. "The guard ran off and left them in the doorknob."

He unlocked his mother's door and slid it opened, revealing the foot of a bed and a desk with no chair, but he didn't see his mother. His heart pounded in his chest. Where could she be? Poking his head all the way into the room, he caught a movement out of the corner of his eye.

A voice came from the same direction. "Oh, Henry, I almost hit you!" His mother lowered the chair she had been clutching high in the air.

Knowing they were short on time, Henry kept his emotions in check and refrained from hugging his mother. Instead, he motioned to her to be quiet then ran to his father's room, leaving Shandra to guide his mother down the hall.

Henry unlocked the door of the last guest room and swung it open. His father sat tied to a chair, facing the doorway. Considering what his mother had planned to do with *her* chair, Henry figured they had tied up the wrong Johnson.

As soon as he got the ropes off his father, Henry found himself squashed between his parents in a family hug.

Shandra cleared her throat. "There's no time for a reunion unless you want to stay here."

Reluctantly, Henry stepped away. "Right, you take them to the door. I'm going to put the keys back, so they won't know what happened."

He jogged down to C3 and inserted the key into the lock, leaving the door ajar. When he got back down the hall, Shandra and his parents were huddled beneath the window of the outside door.

He ducked down as a shadow passed the frosted glass. "What's going on?"

Shandra shifted her weight. "The guards are running back and forth. I think Oscar and Tina are doing too good of a job. I texted the code to everyone."

The ongoing danger tempered Henry's relief at finding his parents. "Let's hope they remember what to do."

His father's voice carried both amazement and regret. "You kids shouldn't be here."

Henry patted his father's shoulder. "It was the only way. Don't worry. We have a plan."

More shadows passed the window, and his father asked, "Is there a Plan B?"

"Wait a minute," Shandra said. "We should be able to leave pretty soon."

She'd better be right because Henry's leg muscles were starting to cramp from crouching. He stood at the side of the door to relieve his muscles and get a better view.

The frosted glass prevented him from seeing any more than vague shapes. By the sizes of the shapes and the pattern of the movements, he figured Oscar and Tina were leading the guards all over the grounds.

Chapter 29

Blurry shapes passed in front of Chuck's binoculars and obscured his view. Lowering the glasses, he realized Tina had run across the grass between B and C Wings pursued by a hefty security guard.

Oscar sprinted past a few seconds later with another guard close behind. The guard Chuck had seen leaving the lobby a few moments ago burst out of C Wing and joined the chase.

If the guard had time to chase Oscar and Tina, Henry and Shandra must have been able to hide. Now, thanks to Chuck's quick thinking, they only had Dr. Grey left to worry about.

As planned, Oscar and Tina ran a crisscross pattern across the lawn, confusing the guards. Chuck contributed by giving the guards the idea to chase first one of the children and then the other.

After several minutes, Oscar took the lead and headed around B Wing toward the front of the building. All Chuck could do was watch for Henry and Shandra to bring out the rescued captives.

Looking toward C Wing in hopes of spotting his fellow Tweaks, he saw instead a fourth guard. While

Chuck had been watching the chase, this new guard must have rounded C Wing. Now he stood halfway between Chuck and the Institute, peering at the gardener's shed. He took a step then another—heading straight for the shack.

Chuck froze. His heartbeat pounded in his ears. Self preservation overcame his fear, and he backed away to the chain link fence. Turning, he scrambled half way up. He'd be over it and gone before the guard reached the shed. Then, for the first time in his life, he thought of someone else.

"Karen." The whisper barely escaped his lips. "I promised." He jumped down and faced forward. He needed a diversion—immediately.

His face puckered in concentration, and he envisioned the little fourth grader with the straight hair and weird T-shirt. *Tina, come to the back. Come to the back.*

He waited and listened. Footsteps and heavy breathing drew near.

Tina gasped for breath between her words. "Can't . . . catch . . . me!"

Chuck threw himself on the ground along the side of the shed as he felt his cell phone vibrate in his shirt pocket. He rolled partway over and reached into his pocket for the phone.

The text screamed one word in capital letters. *NOW*

Army crawling to the front of the shed, Chuck risked a peek. The new guard had turned to join the pursuit. Tina dodged within several feet of him and circled the end of C Wing with Oscar and all four guards trailing.

Chuck made his way to the back of the shed. Karen, still and empty of her consciousness, lay where he'd left her.

"I'm sorry," he whispered. "I almost deserted you." He reached out to her with his mind. *Come back.*

Karen stirred then opened her eyes and smiled. "Hi. What's going on?"

"Shandra just texted the signal. It's time to go meet up with Jim."

She crawled out from behind the shed, and he helped her stand. She paused on wobbly legs, leaning on him for support. "I need a second." Karen shook one foot and then the other. "Okay, I'm ready."

Chuck checked to make sure the yard was still empty, and then they ran toward the bushes along B Wing. Ducking behind the hedge at the corner, Chuck collided with Jim as he scooted backwards to make room for them.

Checking the other end of the wing with the binoculars, Chuck couldn't tell if Dr. Grey still sat at his computer. They'd better hurry. He sent thoughts about Mapleton toward Dr. Grey's office, just in case.

Turning his head toward Karen, Chuck whispered, "Jim and I'll stay here and help. Work your way back to the van. Tell your brother to be ready."

Karen sprinted to the other side of B Wing and slid behind the azaleas. With her gone, Chuck concentrated on Oscar, picturing his black glasses and unruly hair. *Work your way around D Wing.*

*   *   *

Henry watched the ghostly game of tag through the frosted glass. "Okay, they went around the corner. Let's wait half a minute to make sure they don't come back again."

Shandra bobbed her head in agreement.

Counting the seconds in a whisper, Henry motioned to the others to scoot back away from the door, so he could open it a crack and peek outside.

He reached for the handle but caught his breath as the door began to open on its own. He looked at Shandra. She shook her head and mouthed, "It's not me."

With the lights on, all the nearby doors locked, and the keys way down the hall, they had nowhere to hide. They split into two groups and plastered themselves against the walls on either side of the door. Henry found himself between the widening crack and his mother. They should have brought her chair along.

As the crack grew larger, Henry spied a hand clutching the outer doorknob. Were the guards armed? He motioned to his dad to move out away from the wall a little.

If he could pull the guard into the hall, he'd need his dad ready to pounce. The opening widened enough for him to reach through. He moved to snatch the hand, but the sight of a jagged scar on the thumb stopped him.

Grabbing the edge of the door instead, Henry pulled it open to reveal his best friend. "Jim, it's us."

"Oh!" Jim exhaled a rush of air. "You scared me."

Shandra stepped around the door. "Let's go!"

They all followed Jim outside and toward B Wing where Chuck hunkered behind a bush.

Henry tilted his chin up. "Hey."

Holding up one finger to quiet Henry, Chuck used his other hand to wave them toward the waiting van. Henry didn't risk breaking Chuck's concentration any further. He motioned to his parents and pointed to the van on the street where Mr. Goetz had the engine idling, ready for a bank-robbery-style getaway.

They took a quick look around the corner of B Wing to make sure the front lawn was empty before sprinting toward the vehicle. As they approached, the side door of the van flew open, and Karen slid out.

Henry's father looked from Mr. Goetz to Karen and then turned to his son.

"Not now, Dad. Don't worry; they're with us. I'll explain later."

Henry's father shrugged and followed the others into the van.

Henry reached out to help his mother, but she backed away. "I'm not going anywhere until you explain."

"Later." Henry's eyes darted toward the Institute. "We've got to go, Mom."

Before she could respond, the front door opened, and the receptionist rushed out with a cell phone in her hand. She looked down the street and stopped when she noticed them. "Hey, does Dr. Grey know you're out here?"

As Henry urged his mother forward, a loud clatter sounded from out on the street followed by an awful, scraping noise. A lime green Volkswagen bug eased around the van and parked in front of it with its front fender dragging on the pavement.

The receptionist rushed toward the car. "Derrik, look what you've done to my baby!"

Henry used the distraction to propel his mother into the van and jump in behind her. The door swung shut thanks to Shandra, and Mr. Goetz stomped on the gas.

The van jerked forward, and Henry stumbled, tripping on Jim's foot. He lurched forward and sprawled across Shandra's lap. Springing up, he installed himself on the seat between Shandra and Jim.

As the van sped toward the corner, Henry's mother yelled from the backseat, "The others!"

Henry groaned. "Mom, we still have a plan. We're just going around the block."

Sitting back, Henry's mother stared out the window. "But the receptionist."

Jim snickered. "Don't worry. She's so mad at her boyfriend . . ."

Going into mind reading stance, Henry squinted then nodded. "She's forgotten all about you."

They circled three quarters of the way around the block and pulled up next to a convenience store that backed the Institute. From there, they had a view of the side grounds where Oscar and Tina still played hide and seek with four guards.

"Look." Shandra pointed at the shrubs at the far corner of D Wing. Henry could just make out Chuck creeping along, making his way around the building.

At that moment, one of the guards grabbed Oscar and shook him. Tina looked toward her captured accomplice and stopped, allowing another guard to snatch her arm.

Despair filled Henry's mother's voice. "Oh, no! They've got them."

Shandra's eyes grew wide. "This is *not* part of the plan. Why did Tina let them catch her, too?"

Karen wrinkled her nose. "I don't know, but those little kids better not rat us out."

Each detained by one of the guards, Tina and Oscar looked at the ground, nodding their heads, as one of the men shook his finger at them.

Jim edged closer to the window. "Oscar's scared, really scared, but Tina's excited."

Henry kneeled on the seat to get a better look. "I'm picking up her vision of what's going to happen next. It's all right. Watch."

On the lawn, Oscar said something and pointed down the road. The guards released them, and they ran across the grass toward the van. When they reached the street, they passed the vehicle containing their friends.

Jim turned in his seat to watch them. "Where are they going?"

Tuning in on the small girl, Henry closed his eyes. "Tina says they'll wait for us two blocks down."

The pair headed down the sidewalk, out of sight of the guards, but the van stayed put.

Henry's father stared out the tinted window. "Charles is still out there."

The guards watched until Tina and Oscar were well out of view. Then they turned toward D Wing and started across the lawn in the direction of Chuck's hiding place. Henry's mother gasped but said nothing.

Twenty feet from Chuck, the lead guard stopped. After a short pause, he turned back to his companions, and Henry could tell he was saying something to them. After a brief discussion, they turned in unison and headed back toward C Wing.

Henry cued in on the head guard's thoughts and then slapped his knee. "Chuck must have sent them to check the gardener's shed."

171

When the guards were safely around the corner, Mr. Goetz eased the van forward, and Chuck jumped up from behind the hedge.

At that moment, the door to C Wing was flung open, and Dr. Grey barreled out, flapping his arms in the air.

Karen laughed. "He waddles like a penguin."

Henry gulped. "If you could hear his thoughts, you wouldn't laugh." He glanced at his mother. "He knows you've escaped. He's thinking, 'I'll find her. No more persuasion. If she won't talk, I'll force it out of her.'"

As he went, Dr. Grey's head swung one way then the other. When he faced the guards, he yelled and motioned to them. All four men spun around and rushed forward.

At Dr. Grey's shout, Chuck stopped in his tracks and looked first at the van and then back at his hiding place in the hedge.

Henry gauged the time before the men would see Chuck. "He's got about four seconds to decide."

It didn't take Chuck that long. He dashed toward the van.

Henry picked up Chuck's projected plea. *Karen, help me.*

Karen swung the van door open and jumped out. "Run!"

The five men jerked their heads toward the sound. Dr. Grey's face turned red. "Get them. Get them all."

The guards raced toward Chuck, who lowered his head and pumped his arms harder as he ran. The forward-most guard leaped at Chuck. In mid tackle, his body flew sideways and thudded to the ground. The other three guards stumbled, caught up by a tree branch that skidded across the grass.

Shandra collapsed into her seat. "Take that!"

The van crept forward. Karen and Chuck flew through the open door as Henry slammed it shut. Chuck closed his eyes and wrinkled his brow. "One more hint we're from Mapleton."

Tina grinned. "Great job! We bought the van there, and the license plate holder says, 'Mapleton Car Mart.'"

Mr. Goetz stepped on the accelerator, and the van sped away. Henry peered out the back window as Dr. Grey stamped the ground and screamed at the pile of guards at his feet.

Jim pumped his hand in the air. Chuck, Henry and Shandra followed suit and all shouted in unison, "Tweak 'em."

Karen slumped against the window. "He saw me."

Chapter 30

They circled the block and found Oscar and Tina waiting on a corner down the street. With all ten of them in the van, everyone seemed to relax until Henry's father let out a sound filled with doom. "Oh, no."

He put his hand on his forehead. "I didn't want Dr. Grey to have access to my car, so I left it down the street from the Institute yesterday!" His eyes grew wide. "We can't go get it. It's too close, and they saw the van."

Henry hoped the circumstances justified the broken family rules he was about to confess. "I used the keypad on the door to get in the car and get your spare key out of the glove box. Mr. Goetz moved the car down the street before we came to get you."

"There it is." Jim pointed at the blue sedan parked in front of a hardware store.

Mr. Goetz pulled in beside the car and looked at Henry's parents in the rear view mirror. "We need to put more distance between us and the Institute before we explain everything to you." He turned to face them. "Follow us. I know a place where we can talk."

Henry was torn between going with his parents and staying with the Tweaks. He felt like a star quarterback being pulled away from the victory celebration.

Jim elbowed Henry's arm. "I'll go with Henry and his parents, but don't say *anything* until we're all back together!"

"Gotcha," Karen agreed for the group. "You bring Henry's parents up to speed."

The boys followed Henry's parents to their car, and Henry playfully shoved Jim in. Even though Jim sometimes grumbled that his ability wasn't very impressive, it sure helped having a best friend who understood how he felt.

After winding through the city streets for ten minutes, Henry's father and Mr. Goetz slid into adjacent spaces in the parking lot at Roosevelt Park. The spring sun hung much lower than half-mast, but they'd have at least another hour of daylight—enough to unwind and debrief before heading back to Riverton.

The Tweaks and the three adults converged on the biggest table in the picnic area. With Mr. Goetz sitting in the middle of one side across from Henry's parents, Henry felt trapped in a parent-teacher conference.

Mr. Goetz cleared his throat. "I met with the other parents last night and explained who I am. I assume Henry has filled you in."

Henry's father offered his hand. "Yes, he has. I thought there was something familiar about you. Your dad and I used to fish on the river together."

175

"I remember. He hated to move away. They were just so worried about Karen." Mr. Goetz shifted his gaze to Henry's mother. "They deserted your experiment, and I wouldn't blame you if you—"

Henry's mother cut him off. "I understand. Your mother knew Karen's ability would be of the most interest to the Institute." She patted Karen's hand. "I'm glad I didn't know about you sooner. If Dr. Grey had used drugs on me . . ." She shuddered. "It would only make him more determined to find all of you if he knew one of you could project. Imagine the harm the wrong person could cause with that ability."

Karen smiled up at her. "He didn't use the drugs, and we all got out of there safely. That's the important thing." She looked at her brother and frowned. "But he saw me. He saw Chuck, too, but he saw my *face*."

Mr. Goetz nodded. "I know, but I don't think he'd recognize you if he saw you again. It all happened very quickly."

"About that," Henry's father interjected, "I'd like to hear more about this 'plan.'"

Henry grinned. "Sorry, I didn't have time to tell you everything back there."

It took ten minutes for the whole story to come out because whenever anyone started to tell it, someone else jumped in with their part. When they finished, Henry's father ran through it again, as if to check his understanding. "So Mr. Goetz and Jim caused a disturbance at the front door to draw most of the guards

176

there while Henry and Shandra sneaked in. Then Tina and Oscar occupied the guards by pretending to be neighborhood kids playing on the grounds."

He pointed at each of them as he worked his way around the table. "Chuck helped confuse the guards by putting conflicting thoughts in their heads. Karen popped in and out, so to speak, to keep track of everyone and learn more about Dr. Grey's plans, and Henry and Shandra pulled off the commando rescue."

"That's about it," Mr. Goetz agreed. "We've got a long drive home. Why don't you kids go—"

Not stopping to hear the rest, the Tweaks raced to the playground like captives set free.

As Henry hopped up from the table, he heard Mr. Goetz address his parents. "We need to talk."

Chapter 31

The Tweaks relived the daring rescue once again for the benefit of the Riverton Book Club the next day in Shandra's spacious living room over potluck brunch. Henry sat near his mother, the club's founding member and favorite author, who regarded the Tweaks, as each, in turn, related his or her part of the mission.

Her unusual silence worried Henry, and he probed her mind to find her thoughts revolved around the children she'd known since birth. *They've grown so much in the last two days. My gifts to them have helped them mature. But they've also stolen their childhood.*

Henry was concentrating on his mother's thoughts so intently he didn't realize she had stood and was now speaking out loud. "I can't tell you kids how grateful we are you rescued us." She reached down to hold her husband's hand as she spoke. "However, there are some things Karen learned yesterday we haven't shared with you yet."

She looked around the room at the people whose lives she had helped sculpt. "I realize now Dr. Grey would have used any means to make me expose you. Thanks to Karen, we know he will keep searching for the children. He believes we are in this general area, and he suspects I have a child with an ability. Chuck steered him toward Mapleton, so we should have a couple of weeks, but that's all."

She paused and scanned the faces of her audience. "I think the only solution is for each family to move somewhere else as soon as possible."

She let the implications of this statement sink in. Henry's mouth fell open, and he exchanged a fearful glance with Jim.

Shandra was more vocal. "We can't do that!"

Even Chuck seemed agitated by the idea of losing the bond that had so recently developed between the seven Tweaks. He looked from one of them to another and ended by staring at Karen with a wrinkled brow.

Taking a deep breath, Henry's mother spoke forcefully. "It's the only way to keep all of you safe."

Oscar took off his glasses and wiped them on his T-shirt. "My dad already talked to his aunt in Florida. We're leaving as soon as school ends."

Henry cringed against the explosion of sound that followed. Chuck's mother's voice rose above the others. "What will we do? Where will we go?"

Chuck glared at her through squinted eyes, and she glanced at him, surprised, but she sat and shut her mouth. Henry gave Chuck a grateful look. He didn't like it that Chuck could give him ideas, but controlling his mother's hysterics seemed a good use for his ability.

Mr. Goetz took advantage of the relative quiet. "I may have another solution." He waited for the rest of the noise to die down. "I know how difficult this is for all of you, and I am beginning to understand how hard it was for my parents to leave here."

He pointed at the kids around the room. "After watching them in action, I think it would be better for your children if they were able to stay together. If you all move to different towns, maybe they'd be safer, maybe not. For sure, they'd be different. Alone."

Everyone nodded except Chuck's mother. Her eyes were wide. "What are you suggesting?"

"My parents owned a farm about a hundred miles from here. Karen and I inherited it. I'd like to start a boarding school there for your children. I have to finish my teaching contract, and, it would attract too much attention if all the kids withdrew from school at the same time, especially this late in the year. I think we can stay here for these last two weeks of school if the kids can refrain from using their abilities in public."

He gave Chuck a stern look that brought a howl of laughter from the other kids. "Immediately after school ends, we must move the kids to the new school. You parents could come and visit anytime, and the kids and their gifts would be away from inquisitive eyes."

Chucks mother gasped. "You mean . . ."

Again, Chuck peered at his mother, but she shook her head at him. "That won't work again, Charles. I can't let you leave me, not yet." She turned back to Mr.

Goetz. "Are you seriously suggesting we let our children go off and live with you on this farm?"

Shandra's mother stood. "It's either that or split them up and raise them as, as . . ."

"As freaks," Chuck finished for her. "Don't you see, Mom? I've been a bully my whole life because I got the idea, *from you*, that I was special. I thought anything I did was okay merely because I thought it." He shifted his eyes toward the other Tweaks, tilted his head, and gave a little shrug, almost as if apologizing.

Chuck turned back to his mother. "If I'm out there on my own, I *am* special, but it's not a good kind of special." He pointed around the room at the other kids. "With them, I'm just Chuck. I'm not a freak. I'm a. . ."

Six other voices chimed in, "Tweak!"

In the end, Oscar's father had the last word on the subject. "I know Oscar wouldn't choose to leave his family, but I've never seen him happier than he's been this week. I'm willing to let him go if that's what it takes for him to be happy . . . and safe."

Henry moved to sit between his parents. It seemed everything he'd ever known was coming to an end. Then he noticed the excitement dancing in Tina's eyes. She winked at him, and for just a moment, he picked up a glimmer of the thrill that awaited them in exploring a new place with the freedom to practice their abilities. This might be an ending of sorts, but it was also . . .

The Beginning

If you'd like to help introduce Henry and the rest to others, please post a review on Goodreads and/or Amazon. These reviews help readers know if they would like a book, and they help the author reach more potential readers.

To follow the continuing adventures of the Tweaks, try out this sample Book Two:

Tweaks

The Grey Ops

Chapter One

Riverton Elementary school's library had never felt so evil. Jim Forbes stepped through the doorway and looked around. His sixth grade classmates headed into the annual book fair with mixed emotions. He zeroed in on Bruce, the most likely to harbor the icy emotion Jim was feeling. All he got from the would-be terrorist was boredom.

The girl next to him oozed excitement as she studied a poster of the latest teen heartthrob. The librarian exuded impatience, but she wasn't the cause of the cold darkness he felt creeping through his body. He pasted his usual grin on his face to mask his growing nervousness and moved farther into the library. The feeling ebbed like the tide pulling away from the shore, leaving only a foamy residue in its wake.

The person harboring the menacing emotions must be down the hall. He hoped whoever it was stayed there. He usually had to be within a few feet of someone to "read" the person's emotions. He'd never encountered feelings strong enough to reach out to him from the next room. The sooner he got out of the main building and back to the sixth grade portable, the better.

Grabbing the book he wanted, he got in the cashier line with his best friend, Henry Johnson. As the line crept in the direction of the hall, he wondered if the unwanted emotion would return.

He joked with Henry, hoping his own good humor would protect him from the nasty feeling. He stepped forward, and the chill crept through him again. The person containing the wickedness he kept feeling must still be in one of the classrooms nearby.

Jim hated this ability to feel others' emotions he'd inherited from his mother. If he had to have his genes tweaked in a scientific experiment, at least he could have gotten something less girly, something useful. This empathy thing was totally worthless.

He knew someone nearby felt an overpowering hate, but he didn't know who or why. It could be the teacher in the classroom at the top of the stairs had fought with her husband that morning. Maybe that kid working on his math in the hall despised his teacher for sending him there. Jim tried to push the more troubling possibilities out of his mind.

As the girl in front of him moved toward the cashier, a ripple of anticipation reached out to him, reminding him how much he wanted the book in his hands. Even this pleasant emotion irritated him. Why couldn't he enjoy his own feelings without having to deal with the invading sentiments of everyone around him? He turned toward Henry. "I can't wait to read this."

Henry took the book and read part of the back cover blurb. "Follow the crew while they plan and produce an episode of *Blake Savage, Teen Operative*, the smash hit about the high school junior who doubles as a sophisticated undercover agent." Henry turned the book over, exposing the picture of Blake, dressed in black, sneaking through a doorway. "I wish my mom would let me watch it."

"Why won't she?"

Henry shrugged. "For one thing, she says it's not believable a teenager would get to be a spy."

Jim lowered his voice. "She tweaked our mother's genes to turn us into mutants with special abilities, and she doesn't believe a teenager could do intelligence work?"

When Henry only shrugged again, Jim resumed his normal tone. "Besides, he didn't just 'get to be a spy.'" Jim tapped the book for emphasis. "It kind of happened by accident. This clandestine operative, code named

Ferret, had to leave some information at a dead drop for another agent to pick up."

Henry looked confused, and Jim felt the coolness of his friend's negative emotion.

"A dead drop is a place where operatives leave messages for each other."

When Henry nodded, Jim picked up where he'd left off. "Anyway, the drop was a compartment on a motor scooter parked in front of a certain building. When Ferret got there, a truck was parked in front of the scooter, so he couldn't see it."

"So, what did he do?"

"That's just it. Blake Savage's scooter looked exactly like the hidden one, so Ferret put the message in Blake's scooter by mistake."

Henry's puzzled look returned. "But how did that get Blake to be a spy?"

Jim corrected him. "A clandestine operative."

"Whatever. How did he get to be one?"

"When Ferret realized his error, he tracked down Blake, but so did the enemy operative, who'd been watching the drop. Blake and Ferret ended up working together to get the information to the right people and escape from the bad guy."

"Oh," Henry said, "so that's how he got started?"

"Yeah, Blake did so well Ferret brings him in on other operations when he needs help. The rest of the time, he goes to high school and stuff."

Henry opened the book to the index. "Look at all this spy talk. I know *humint* means intelligence gathered by humans, but what is *imint*?"

"The int means intelligence. The im is for imagery, so it's information gathered by satellites." Jim pointed at the page. "Sig is for signal, so *sigint* is from tapping phones. It's all real spy stuff."

Henry nudged his friend. "You mean clandestine operative stuff."

Jim's shoulders sagged. What did Henry know? His mom wouldn't even let him watch the show. A twinge of the icy hatred he'd been feeling nagged at him. Whoever it was hadn't gone away. He tried to block the invading emotion by concentrating on his conversation with Henry. "Why else won't she let you watch it?"

"Mom thinks it's too violent."

Jim perked up. "Nah, it's mostly sneaking around and gathering secrets. He's not much of a fighter. He usually outsmarts the bad guys." Jim pointed at his own head. "Blake uses his brains and his training to get the job done. I'm going to be a spy someday, too."

Giving the book back, Henry looked thoughtful. "Like my dad says, 'If you're a cat, be the best cat you can be. Don't waste time trying to be a dog.'"

"What does that mean?" Jim cocked his head. He tried to envision his cat, Sebastian, chasing a car or digging a hole to hide a bone.

After taking a big breath, Henry hesitated for a moment. "Be yourself. Don't try to be someone else. You're my best friend, not some TV spy."

Jim screwed up his mouth. "But Blake's so smooth. He always knows what to do."

Henry didn't respond but pointed forward. They'd worked their way up to the cashier, and Jim paid for his book. As they lined up to go back to class, Jim pointed to the picture on the cover. "That's Blake Savage. Doesn't he look cool?"

Henry, of course, shrugged, but Jim stared at the picture, wishing he could be more like Blake. Maybe if he could read minds like Henry, he'd have a chance. He couldn't imagine Blake saving the day with empathy. Feeling someone else's emotions didn't fit on a spy's resume.

Looking up, Jim glanced through the double glass doors to the top of the stairs. The iciness he'd been feeling turned glacial, only he knew the source of this emotion—himself. Freezing fear paralyzed him as he watched their principal, Mrs. Smothers, lead a short, thickset man down the hall toward the library. As they approached, Jim snapped out of his stupor. He grabbed Henry's arm and dragged him behind the nearest bookshelf.

Henry pulled away. "What are you doing? We're supposed to line up when we're done buying."

"Dr. Grey." It was all Jim could spit out.

"Huh?" Henry stared at him. "Dr. Grey from the Institute?"

"Yeah." Taking a steadying breath, Jim forced the explanation past the lump in his chest. "He's headed this way with Mrs. Smothers."

Henry peeked around the edge of the bookcase and jerked his head back again. "What'll we do?"

Jim's own fear of the greedy scientist only made him feel Henry's terror all the more. When the hatred he'd felt earlier eased its way around the bookcase, he led Henry into the reference section without thinking. Putting distance between himself and Dr. Grey made the feeling subside a little, and his brain recovered. "What's he doing here?"

"Dunno." Henry crouched behind a set of dictionaries. "Let's find Mr. Goetz."

The boys crept between the fiction and biography areas until they could see the last of their classmates browsing the book fair. Their long term substitute, Mr. Goetz, urged the slowpokes to make their selections.

Jim kept his voice low. "Psst."

Their teacher scanned the area. Jim repeated the sound, a little louder. Mr. Goetz rounded the shelves between them. "What are you two doing back here?"

Both boys shushed their teacher. Jim waved him closer then whispered, "We saw Dr. Grey." He pointed toward the door.

Mr. Goetz took a step back and glanced toward the door. His face lost all color, and his mouth formed a stiff line. "They're headed down the main stairs. You boys get in the end of our line, and I'll take us down the back stairs."

Jim and Henry obeyed, each feeling the foreboding of a condemned man on his way to the gallows.

Look for further volumes of this series at Aamazon.com.

Future titles include:
Tweaks: The Grey Ops
Tweaks: The Destiny School

About the Author

Terry Deighton lives in Washington, the state not D.C., with her husband, Al. Their six children are grown and gone, and pets tend to complicate life. When she is not writing and revising, again, she works as a substitute teacher. Mr. Goetz is wiser and cooler, but he's made up, so it doesn't count. Mrs. Deighton started out to be a high school English teacher, but raising kids turned into a fulltime job. During those years, her dream of writing books for young people grew until she had to do something about it. You are holding the fulfillment of that dream.

To contact her and for information of future titles, visit www.tweaksthebeginning.wordpress.com or www.amazon.com/author/terrydeighton.